SIEMPRE
TESSA CÁRDENAS

Dreamspinner Press

Published by
Dreamspinner Press
5032 Capital Circle SW
Suite 2, PMB# 279
Tallahassee, FL 32305-7886
USA
http://www.dreamspinnerpress.com/

This is a work of fiction. Names, characters, places, and incidents either are the product of author imagination or are used fictitiously, and any resemblance to actual persons, living or dead, business establishments, events, or locales is entirely coincidental.

Siempre
© 2013 Tessa Cárdenas.

Cover Art
© 2013 Paul Richmond.
http://www.paulrichmondstudio.com
Cover content is for illustrative purposes only and any person depicted on the cover is a model.

ISBN: 978-1-62798-309-9
Digital ISBN: 978-1-62798-308-2

Printed in the United States of America
First Edition
December 2013

DEDICATION

Dedicated with love to John and Lani.

John, without you, this book would not be here, because I would not be here. I can't even put into words all the ways you've saved me.

Lani, there are so many things I could say about your unwavering love and friendship, but in the end, what stands out more than anything is that when I'm with you, I always feel so incredibly alive. You know how special that is.

ACKNOWLEDGMENTS

Additional thanks to everyone who helped make this book happen so quickly.

Steph, for all your help every step of the way from the planning, to writing, to editing. I never would have finished anything again without you.

Lani and Ryan, thanks for enabling my love affair with New York City by letting me visit so many times.

Serena, for enduring long e-mails full of questions about Purchase and photography and then forgiving me when all that work showed up in only a few sentences.

My mom, for checking and editing all my Spanish while conveniently not asking awkward questions about context.

Stacy, Linda, Mary, and Nessa, for help with final editing and proofreading so no one knows how many words and commas I forget.

CHAPTER 1

SEAN LET himself fall down on the black marley flooring of the studio. The smooth rubber felt cool enough on his back that he didn't mind the sour smell as he turned his head to press his cheek to the floor. His blond hair had long ago given up on the short spikes he'd started the day with, forcing him to push back the sweaty strands from his forehead.

"Get up. Stretch," Travis ordered, nudging Sean's ankle with his foot as Sean's dance partner Alana ignored him and collapsed next to Sean.

"Fine. Be lazy. Get muscle cramps. You have understudies." Travis shook his head and turned to wander back to the sound system in the corner of the room.

"Our understudies are going to be junior-year college interns who only get hounded by you once or twice a week. Even if a prodigy shows up at the audition today, you would have to break labor laws to feel like they rehearsed enough for you," Alana said, but she still raised her hands above her head as she pointed her toes, stretching her whole body horizontally before sitting up and folding herself in half.

"They'll probably complain less."

"Because they'll be scared of you," Sean said as he followed Alana's example. He might not fear Travis, but he knew well enough that he'd curse himself in the next day's classes and rehearsals if he didn't start stretching.

"Which is why I'll like them better." Travis pulled an envelope out of his bag and carried it over to where Sean and Alana were stretching on the floor. Alana shifted so Travis had space to pull out the glossy eight-by-tens and spread them out in the middle of their small circle.

"Are we picking favorites before we've even see them?" Sean asked as Alana began sliding the women to the left side of the circle and the men to the right.

"Just getting ideas." Travis slid three of the women and three of the men to the top. "These six have the best résumés. Years of classes, summer programs, leads in productions. I'm not sure why they even went to college."

"So you hate them already?" Sean rolled his eyes at Alana, and Travis shrugged. "You realize that you would have automatically rejected your best friend from this company if you'd been in charge at our audition."

"No. I'm just saying they'll have plenty of opportunities at plenty of companies. If we want them, we need to grab them fast. Why do you think you got your call the next day, and I got mine a week later?" Travis said. "I haven't written them off. I can't, anyway. Steph is still the director, and you know she'd overrule me if I tried. She offered you a place because she knew that you were a good fit for the company, but we want interns we can develop—not interns who will take their credit and never come back. We're not ABC. We can't just train interns and not care if they take that training elsewhere."

Sean nodded as he skimmed over the six résumés while Travis pushed six more to the lower end of the spread.

"Least experience?" Alana asked, and Travis nodded.

Sean glanced over and waved his hand for Alana to continue.

"Say it. I know you want to," he said when she stayed silent.

"I don't have to say it. But if you have danced with me for two years and you need me to point out that all the white people are on the top, with long lists of classes and lead roles, and the black and brown people are on the bottom, I'm going to kick you in the face the next time we do that lift." Alana didn't look away from the résumé she'd picked up to read as she added, "Accidentally, of course."

"And yet you always pick on me about it and not Travis."

"Because Travis knows he's white."

"I have looked in a mirror."

"And yet you keep trying to think it doesn't matter."

Travis picked up the picture she'd just put down and handed it to Sean, saving him from answering. The girl in the picture held a first arabesque en pointe like every other dancer, but he could see how she was probably a few inches too short by regular ballet standards, and her hips set just a little wider than would be ideal. Her form was still close to perfect, but when he flipped the picture over, he wasn't surprised to find that even with the short list of leading roles from her Arizona dance school, Guadalupe Torres only had one small solo and various corps performances since she'd started studying at Purchase College's dance conservatory two years ago.

"Only you would have a favorite from just a picture." Sean shook his head but flipped the photo back to the front. If anyone could pick a dancer from a picture, it would be Travis. Travis was worried that Steph had started passing off control of the company to him out of pity when his knee surgery had ended his dance career, but Sean knew it had only sped up the process. Travis had an eye for finding talent other people might pass by. He had insisted on getting Alana into an audition after he'd spotted her go-go dancing in a nightclub two years ago, and he hadn't been wrong there.

"That's why I also want your opinions."

"Even though you'll pick who you want after you listen to them?" Alana said, but her smile gave away her trust. She glanced at the clock and pointed before reaching her hand out to Sean to help her up before he'd even gotten up himself. He rolled his eyes but still stood and took her hand to pull her up before moving to help Travis set up a folding table and chairs for them to make notes. Alana tossed the pointe shoes she'd already removed toward her bag, and pulled on soft ballet shoes to lead the students through the audition.

Sean and Travis had just settled at the table when the receptionist poked her head in the door. At Travis's nod, she came into the studio with a list of names and numbers, followed by a small group of dancers whom Alana directed into lines according to number. He recognized

Guadalupe right away and caught Travis's slight smile as she lined up in front with a "#1" pinned to the front of her leotard. If she hadn't already caught Travis's eye with her résumé, he knew she'd get points for showing up early enough to get the first number.

As Alana led the dancers through exercises, Sean had to admit that Guadalupe stood out. Travis had instructed Alana to start them with classical ballet to highlight their technique and flexibility, but even then, they were looking for someone who naturally added their own spirit. As they moved into more modern combinations, Guadalupe's passion showed through even more. He almost forgot to watch for the male dancers—something he was sure Travis would tease him for, if he knew.

It only took a few shared nods and expressions between the three of them to realize Travis had mostly decided on his original pick and needed to see how the males danced with her, so Alana taught them a section of the dance they'd been rehearsing an hour earlier. She had each of the dancers trade partners for various parts as all three of them tried to find a guy who would fit the part and the company. It was obvious Alana was trying to pair Guadalupe with the males she thought Travis would like, but Sean found his eye kept catching on number eight. His classical technique was perfect, but he was struggling with the more modern parts of the piece. As he waited on the side for his turn, he worked on the same pose over and over until he got closer. Sean leaned over to write "#8" on Travis's notes. Travis glanced at the dancer and back down to pull his picture.

It was from the first six they'd mostly ignored earlier. A quick glance showed that, before he'd started college, Michael had even attended some of the same summer programs Sean had on his own résumé. Travis gave him an odd look, but he still signaled for Alana's attention and tapped the picture when she looked down.

Alana gave Travis and then Sean a look, but paired Michael with Guadalupe on the next rotation. They surprised him by sharing a smile, and he glanced down at both résumés, noticing that they both went to Purchase. Of course, half the kids auditioning had probably heard of the smaller company, because Travis had landed his spot right after graduating from Purchase.

The kid still stumbled through some of the harder moves, but Sean could see even Alana was nodding at the way the two played off each other. When they finished, she tried a few more combinations just in case they needed to remember some other options, but after they'd dismissed the dancers, she only waited until they were all out of earshot before saying, "Okay. Just call the girl first. No rushing after him and working it out and making her wait a week. She's more likely to stay on with us after, and you know it."

"IT SEEMS kind of cruel and unusual to make them take their first company class from Travis," Alana said. She nodded toward the corner of the room, where the two new interns were stretching together after the last combination before going through it all over again in the opposite direction. "And I think he planned it to be a modern class so he could make Michael cry."

"We could let them know it only gets easier from here?" Sean wiped the sweat off his forehead as Alana fixed a clip in her hair. She'd started the class with her thick black hair in a perfect bun, but now the sweat was making it curl around her hairline.

"Except they have to learn his chorography Saturday too, so they really only get the one break on Thursday with Steph." Alana glanced over to where Travis was correcting a soloist's form. "He's worse today. You live with him. Give him some kind of tranquilizer before rehearsal tomorrow. I'll get it for you, and you can slip it in his breakfast."

"Why are you his favorite?"

"Why are you his best friend? Get the man a girlfriend or something," Alana whispered and forced a smile when Travis glared in her direction. "He needs to get laid."

"So have sex with him."

"Gross. It'd be like having sex with my brother," Alana said as they stepped up to begin the combination for the last time.

Even though he was exhausted, Sean threw himself into every move, somehow letting his body carry him through until the final jump on the other side of the room. Turning, he let himself lean against the barre against the wall next to Alana as the interns forced themselves through it.

Alana reached out to catch Michael's arm before he could slide down the wall.

"Don't. If you're not standing, he'll probably make you do it again. And she'll have to do it again with you." Alana smirked when Michael stood up quickly. "Michael and Guadalupe, right?"

"Lupe," the girl corrected Alana in a whisper with a nervous glance at Travis.

"Right. I'll let him know for you. He likes to yell the correct name when he thinks you're slacking." Alana smirked as they moved to the floor to cool down. There was a reason Sean had to be the nice one in their group.

Sean dropped to the floor to stretch when Travis declared class over. Lupe and Michael only followed suit when Alana waved to indicate it was safe.

"Is every class like this?" Michael asked.

"He's the worst—which is why you guys are lucky and get to work with him twice a week like us. His classes are at the end of the day, because no one can take another after, and those happen to be two of the three that fit in the time that your school schedules allow. Lucky you." Alana's grin only grew at Michael's groan.

"But we *are* lucky. I mean, you guys are the best, right? That's why you have the piece he choreographed. And we actually get to learn it from him. He's like"—Lupe ducked her head with a slight blush—"kind of amazing."

"Lupe saw him dance five years ago when she was visiting her cousin. Then she told her parents she wanted to go to Purchase because it was near New York and her cousin goes there. She really just went because the great Travis Campbell went there. She's been practicing every piece he ever did since freshmen year so she could get this internship." Michael ducked from Lupe's slap and laughed.

"Oh god, shut up. I have no idea how you got it too. You're going to be lucky if he can teach you to not dance like a robot." Lupe turned back to them with red blotches showing through her tan skin. "Please, please don't tell him any of that."

Sean was debating admitting that he would probably tell Travis anyway when the door to the studio opened. A tall man leaned in and looked around. He was too stocky to be a dancer, but then, if he had been in the company, Sean would have met him already. His white tank top contrasted with his tan skin and stretched across his muscular chest and left little to Sean's imagination. His eyes caught Sean's for a second, and he smirked at the obvious attention and offered enough of a nod to let Sean know he didn't mind before letting his eyes drift over Sean's frame in return.

"Wow. At least you might be sweaty enough that the extreme drooling is less obvious." Alana's voice broke him out of his thoughts and made Lupe and Michael turn around. Lupe jumped up and headed for the man whose face was schooled into indifference when Sean looked back.

"And that would be her cousin Jaime," Michael explained. "Very pretty to look at. Very straight and practically married to his girlfriend. I've been in mourning for two years, but feel free to join me."

Lupe left Jaime at the door and came back to pull Michael to his feet.

"Sorry. My stupid cousin insists on driving us because he thinks I can't come to the city on my own, and he's impatient. You'd think he'd be able to stay occupied in all of New York until I call him," Lupe explained as she and Michael gathered their things and pulled on cover-ups.

"Like you want to sit on a train after *that* class," Michael mumbled, casting a wary look at Travis as they left the studio.

Sean waited until they'd all left the room before turning back to Alana.

"That man is not straight. There is no way that man is straight."

"Oh no. This is not happening." Alana stretched to the edge of the room and pulled her phone from her bag to text.

"Stop. Nothing is happening." Sean tried to take the phone, but it wasn't worth getting up, and she stretched her long arms out of his reach.

In less than a minute, Travis came back in the room and joined them on the floor.

"You send the most dramatic texts," he said to Alana. "One day you're going to have a real emergency, and I'm going to laugh at you by accident."

"I realize it's hard for you to switch immediately from your tyrant mode to your best friend mode, but Sean just decided to fall for Lupe's straight cousin."

"He is not straight. There is no way."

Instead of speaking, Alana opted to just wave her hands and point at him instead.

"Okay." Travis glanced between them. "And why does Alana think he is?"

"Because Michael just told us he's practically married to his long-term girlfriend," Alana said before he could say anything.

"And I'm with Alana." Travis sighed, and scratched his short brown hair that was still wet from the shower he'd taken while they stayed behind to talk. "If you are right about him being gay, it looks like he's in the closet. You do *not* want to do that."

"Maybe Michael is wrong." Sean bit his lip and avoided their eyes when he said it, but he hadn't made up that look. Jaime hadn't looked confused or upset. He'd openly smirked and made it obvious he was checking Sean out.

"Oh dear lord. He didn't even speak to the guy. I hope you're ready to have him moping and pining all over your apartment."

CHAPTER 2

SEAN WASN'T proud that he was hanging around outside the studio on Thursday before Steph's level-four ballet class on the one day he could have made it home early. He wasn't proud he'd told Alana he was going to work with one of the soloists who was struggling so she'd leave without him, knowing that Travis would think Sean had followed her out. As it was, they'd find out anyway if Lupe or Michael mentioned seeing him. If Sean was lucky, none of the corps dancers would tell Travis he'd slipped back into the dressing rooms to shower.

He was leaning against the wall scrolling through anything he could think of on his phone when a car pulled up to the curb. Lupe jumped out of the passenger seat, her shiny black hair already pulled into a bun, and she gave him a shy wave as she threw her bag over her shoulder and rushed inside. Michael took one look at him and just shook his head before passing. Sean really needed to come up with a better system, but when the door closed behind Michael and Sean looked up, the car hadn't moved.

Sean pushed off the wall and leaned into the passenger window when it slid down.

"Any chance you can show me a place to park?" Jaime asked, and the sexy smirk Sean remembered was back. He started to point and direct him down the corner, but Jaime reached across the car to pop the passenger door open so Sean could climb in. "I'm Jaime, so you can call me something other than Lupe's annoying overprotective cousin."

"Sean."

"I guess you're already in the company if you don't have to be in this class?" Jaime asked.

"I'm a principal. Company classes are over. They put the interns in a junior company class to match their school schedule. Are you planning to just sit in reception and wait the full two hours?" Sean asked as he directed Jaime to a place his car wouldn't be towed.

"Unless you have a better idea."

"Hungry?"

"I thought my cousin was the only dancer who actually ate." Jaime turned to him with his full smile after he killed the engine.

"I burn it off," Sean answered before opening the car door to get out.

He led the way to a diner a block away where everyone in the company ended up at least once a week to refuel, and the hostess nodded him to a table in the back. As Jaime walked ahead of him, she gave him a quick thumbs-up.

After they ordered and had glasses of water, Sean opened his mouth, only to find himself stopping short and shaking his head instead.

"What?" Jaime asked.

"Am I reading you wrong? Because I don't think I am, but I have to ask."

"Lupe told you I have a girlfriend?" For the first time in the evening, Jaime looked less than confident.

"Michael did."

"I don't. She's my best friend. Somehow, when she became my roommate, my family decided we were dating. I didn't argue." Jaime's eyes flicked to Sean's and then back to where he was gripping his water glass. "I'm not in the closet. My friends know—just not my family. When Lupe decided to go to Purchase, it got complicated."

"And she hasn't figured it out? She's a junior. She's been here a couple years."

"I'm just finishing my last year of grad school. It's a small campus, but not so much that she's going to hear from the visual arts grad students, and almost everyone I did undergrad with moved away before she came." Jaime shrugged. "I know it sounds bad, but I pretty much only see her on the drive here three times a week, and I check in on her once in a while. I'm twenty-five. She's twenty. Trust me, she's not telling me her whole life either, unless she's actually making it through college without getting drunk like she'd have me believe."

"And dinner with me isn't too risky?"

"I wasn't aware you planned to discuss your hookups with the interns." Jaime smiled, but he gave himself away when he bit down on his lip the same way Lupe did when Travis corrected her form.

"I wasn't aware I'd already agreed to a hookup. Maybe I was just hungry, and I felt bad about you sitting around getting bored."

Jaime sat back in his chair and frowned for a second before he realized Sean was struggling to hold back a smile. Then he laughed and leaned forward again.

"Sure. I can let you pretend you just happened to be in the area tonight if you want to play it like that."

SEAN WAS still smiling as he climbed the stairs to the simple two-bedroom apartment he shared with Travis in Brooklyn. Maybe he'd walked away from the diner without a kiss, but only because he was sure that had driven Jaime mad.

He'd just set his duffel down on the floor next to the couch when the door to Travis's room opened. Travis leaned against the doorframe and watched him. When the silence stretched out past the time it took for Sean to pull a bottle of water out of the refrigerator, Sean gave up his plan to pretend nothing had happened.

"He doesn't have a girlfriend."

"She's a beard?" Travis pushed off the doorframe and came to sit on the other side of the couch.

"Just to his family. He's been out for years. He just didn't plan on his cousin seeing you dance at one Purchase event when his family was visiting and becoming so obsessed with you that she insisted on coming all the way across the country with some random hope she could study with you. So really, this new closet is all your fault."

"I'm just going to ignore that you also would never have met him without me and move on to what you don't want to hear."

"He only brings her to classes because her mom thinks she's too young to travel to the city that much on her own. They're from a small town. Her mom thinks the city is full of criminals. Jaime worries about her leaving the city alone when it's dark, so he helps out. She's not so involved in his life that it matters."

"She's involved in *your* life. You shouldn't have to hide a guy from everyone you work with. He'd have to go to shows and pretend he was only there for her. He couldn't see you backstage. He couldn't go to cast parties as your date. So really, you'd be fine going into his world and meeting all his friends, but you'd have to pretend in your own," Travis said.

"It's not that big of a deal."

"You have never even been in a closet. You told your parents you were going to marry Baryshnikov when you were seven, and they were nice enough not to point out your bad taste. You went to a high school for the arts. You don't have any idea."

"You don't either! It's not like you have any kind of experience. Just because you had friends who had it harder than me, doesn't mean you know better than me. You're straight. You can imagine all you want, but that doesn't mean you get it." Sean stood. He'd have to hear the same thing from Alana in the morning, but it would have been nice to enjoy the afterglow of his impromptu date for a few hours. He let the door to his room slam, and for once Travis had the sense not to continue the argument though the door.

"REALLY?" ALANA said, rolling her eyes at him before turning back to the barre. She let her leg slide down the barre until she was in a full side split. "You realize that their rehearsal is after ours, and Travis is going to make sure that by the time Jaime gets here and sees you, you'll be covered in sweat. All your effort to figure out which pants make your ass look the best without looking like you're trying will be wasted."

Sean considered pointing out that Jaime probably wouldn't even see him until after he'd had a chance to shower and change, but then she'd just laugh at how much more ridiculous his efforts were, and she wasn't wrong. Instead, he started his own warm-up without answering.

"We're not going to talk you out of this, are we?" Alana asked after a minute of silence.

"I like him." It might sound like he was thirteen again, but it had been at least a year since a guy had made Sean feel that stupid giddy jump in his chest with each laugh.

"Well then, I guess I might as well admit that if he does get a chance to see you in it, he might not mind the smell with how that tank top is pretty much just painted on. How will you even get that off later? Are you hoping he can just rip it right off your body?"

"More information than I ever needed," Travis deadpanned as he walked through the door and went straight to the stereo to set up the music. Somehow they'd managed to pass each other in the apartment and the studio without really acknowledging each other for the past two days.

"Oh shit." Alana looked from him to Travis and back. "We're both going to die today because you're mad at him, and you think you have to kill us both equally. I have not done anything. I discouraged this from the beginning. I told you about it right away!"

"You both get sloppy on the last set of grands jetés en tournant. They're at the end, and you're tired. Obviously we need to build up your endurance so that stops happening."

You owe me. You owe me so much, Alana mouthed as they finished their warm-up with a series of grands battements en cloche.

Two hours later, Sean was wishing he hadn't decided on a tank top so tight that he couldn't pull it away from his chest to fan the sweat and cool himself off. His water bottle was almost empty enough to not make a mess if he gave up and just dumped the rest over his head. Travis glanced at his watch, but instead of calling the rehearsal finished, he waved them back to their starting position.

"One more time. Do it full-on and you're done. Otherwise I'm sure the interns won't mind you running into their rehearsal. They can watch while they finish warming up."

Later, he was going to point out that they were already running over, and Travis knew that. He opened the door and waved Michael and Lupe into the room so they could see how much they would suffer if Travis decided to continue his wrath with them. It wasn't until they'd finished the full dance that he had a chance to glance at the door and catch a glimpse of Jaime watching through the window. He was rewarded with a small smile before Jaime ducked his head down to the side and disappeared from view.

Alana took a long drink from her own bottle of water and looked to make sure Lupe and Michael were smart enough to give Travis their full attention before leaning close enough to whisper. "Fine. He's adorable. But you still owe me a spa day if rehearsal is like this next week."

Sean nodded as he tried to towel off some of the sweat. He'd been hoping to get a shower before texting Jaime to see if he wanted to kill time together—which was probably exactly why Travis had made sure he was late and sweaty and exhausted. He wasn't even sure he could sit through dinner anywhere. He could maybe manage to stretch to cool down, take a hot shower, and stumble to the subway.

As it was, Jaime was nowhere in sight when he stepped into the hallway. Maybe he'd read the exhaustion off Sean and decided to cut out. They hadn't actually made solid plans. He headed toward the dressing room before Alana could catch up and notice his disappointment.

He was digging in his bag when he noticed the light blinking on his phone and went to check his texts.

Meet me outside where I parked last time?

Sean didn't bother to hide his smile. Travis had made them run late enough that the dressing room was deserted.

Yeah. I just need a shower. 15 minutes?

Jaime's reply came only seconds later.

Sure. Tease. Why don't I live in the city where I can take you home to shower with me?

Sean let his phone fall back into his bag before hurrying through his shower. It was tempting to linger as the hot water ran over his muscles, but they were going to lose time already and if Travis thought about it, he might actually end rehearsal on time. By the time he'd dried off and forced himself into the tight jeans that had seemed like a good idea when he'd tossed them in his bag, it was only an hour and a half before Lupe's rehearsal would be finished.

Outside, Jaime was leaning against his car, fiddling with his phone. Sean had only a few seconds to admire the way the setting sun gleamed off his skin before Jaime noticed him approaching and looked up.

"Hey." Jaime smiled and started to reach for him, then halted. "Are we safe here?"

Sean almost explained that they were in the safest part of Chelsea before he realized Jaime was asking if someone might see them and tell Lupe.

"Yeah. No one else would park here. Everyone else would be going toward the subway."

"Good." Jaime's smile reappeared, and he reached again for Sean's arm to pull him in. "Because I still can't believe you withheld on the first date. Do you have a rule? Because that's very outdated."

He didn't give Sean a chance to answer before he pressed their lips together in a slow kiss Sean couldn't help prolonging as Jaime's hand came up to tangle in the short hair at the base of his neck. When he pulled back, Sean let himself stay pressed against Jaime. He let his lips brush against Jaime's neck before giving in to the rubbery weight of his tired limbs and letting Jaime support more of his weight.

"You're completely dead, aren't you? My chances of talking you into passing the next hour in the backseat of my car are not looking good."

Sean laughed into his neck.

"Even if I ignore that you think I have the standards of a fifteen-year-old with a curfew, there is no way I can cram myself into that space right now."

"That is a ridiculous argument after what I just saw you doing in there. You can most definitely bend in any way necessary," Jaime said, but there wasn't even a hint of annoyance in his voice. He grazed his fingers over Sean's arms, and he pressed a kiss to the top of Sean's head.

"How much did you watch?"

"About three minutes. I have high hopes for your endurance in the future, if that's what you were doing for two hours." Jaime's hand drifted to his waist, where he slipped his fingers under Sean's shirt to skim over bare skin. "It's possible I should have considered how hot you'd make me and how you'd be too tired to enjoy it before I made an excuse to come inside and spy on you."

"It is kind of stalker behavior," Sean said. He pressed closer and let himself relax in Jaime's arms.

"Then we're even for last week." The smile was clear in Jaime's voice as his arms settled around Sean's waist. "You want to stand like this for an hour, or do you live close enough for me to make sure you can get home without falling asleep on the train? I'd drive you, but it's hell enough getting in and out of the city."

"About half an hour?" He really hadn't planned on taking Jaime back to the apartment, but Travis wouldn't be home until after Jaime had to leave anyway.

"So, just enough time to get you there and come back. Can I bargain my way to a real date on the way?"

"You can try."

Jaime laughed as they pulled apart and started the walk to the station.

"Are you always this difficult, or are you just taking advantage of your own exhaustion to act like you are?"

Sean shrugged and decided not to answer. The exasperated look that earned him only made it better even if he gave himself away by snuggling against Jaime as soon as they found seats on the train.

He let himself relax and enjoy Jaime's arm around him as they settled into a comfortable silence. Jaime traced light patterns on his shoulder until they reached his stop.

"You could stay for a few minutes?" Sean said when they reached his door. They only had twenty minutes before Jaime had to go back, but he couldn't help asking.

"I should be worried about myself that I'm going to agree to that when you can barely stand." Jaime shook his head, but followed Sean into the apartment and sat next to him on the couch. "Are rehearsals always that rough? Should I be worried about Lupe's health?"

"Travis is always tough, but he never pushes harder than you can take. He just sometimes pushes right to edge of what I can take." Sean shrugged. "He's kind of mad at me, and he'll be more careful with the kids, anyway."

"He's mad at you, so he takes it out on you in rehearsal?" Jaime's eyes narrowed a bit, and Sean couldn't help jumping to Travis's defense.

"He's worried more than mad. He's just being overprotective in a really annoying way."

"How is working you to exhaustion protecting you from anything?" Jaime asked, but Sean must have given something away with his expression, because he pulled away from Sean and sat back before Sean could come up with an excuse. "Wow. I haven't even really met your best friend, and he hates me already. I think that's a record for me."

"He doesn't hate you."

"So he doesn't think I'm good enough for you, or he wants you for himself?" Jaime frowned when Sean couldn't help chuckling.

"Sorry. It's just that he's straight. Very straight. I'm sure. We've been roommates since a few months after we got into the company six years ago."

"So?"

"So, it's stupid, and I really don't give a shit what he thinks anyway." When Jaime gave him a doubtful look, Sean reached over to pull at his arm. "You have ten minutes before you have to leave. Do you want to spend those ten minutes talking about Travis?"

Jaime laughed and let Sean pull him closer.

"No. But I do want to find out when you'll have more than ten minutes for me."

"Tomorrow? Or next Sunday. Sundays are pretty much always free until we hit our main season."

"I'm good with tomorrow. You want to come up to Purchase? I can take the train here, but in Purchase I can promise a roommate whose not going to cockblock."

"I can make a trip if you're picking me up from the train. I don't bother with having a car here."

"Just give me a time when you figure it out."

Sean nodded before pulling Jaime toward him again. He might be too old to hook up in the back of a car, but he was never going to be above making out on the couch.

SEAN WAS lying in bed trying to read when the familiar knocks on his door came. He'd heard Travis come home an hour earlier, and had decided he'd rather not ruin another good end to his day and face him.

"I'm taking your silence as a cue that you're not jerking off and it's safe to open the door. I'm going to open it now if you don't warn me not to," Travis called through the cheap wood before pushing the door open. He didn't try to enter the room, but he stepped in just enough to lean against the doorframe.

"Have you ever considered that maybe if I wanted to talk to you, I'd actually answer you?"

"No. If you don't want me to come in, you yell at me to go away."

"And you still ignore me." Sean let the book he wasn't reading fall onto the bed. "So say it. Whatever judgment you want to throw at me, go for it."

"I'm not judging. I just don't want to watch you refusing to leave your room and get dressed unless I yell at you like we're in rehearsal. It's disturbing. It makes Alana say we have some kind of relationship I'd really like her to stop trying to explain to me."

"That's not going to happen again."

"There's a pretty high chance." Travis held up his hands before Sean could argue. "But clearly you're not planning on listening to me, and I can't make you. It's your life. And your stupid humane mousetrap has something in it, and if you don't take it out, I'm buying fifteen regular ones and covering them with peanut butter—your shitty organic peanut butter."

CHAPTER 3

SEAN FOUGHT the urge to stand up and pace the narrow aisle of the train car. The ride was only an hour. He'd been stuck on longer subway rides during rush hour that made him curse Travis and his insistence that they live in Brooklyn, but he wasn't usually anticipating a hookup. He hadn't planned a specific place to meet Jaime, but the station at White Plains didn't have many places for him to get lost, anyway. He had only been to Purchase a few times to work with students in the conservatory, and all those times he'd had Travis to lead him around. He was about ten minutes out when his phone buzzed.

This place is boring to kill time in.

Before Sean could think of a reply, it buzzed again.

Not that I was really early. Lexi told me being early would make me look pathetic. There just wasn't any traffic.

Sean fought a grin that would likely make the old lady across the aisle try to start a conversation for the third time.

I'll remember to not mention it to her when I meet her. Am I meeting her?

He wanted to ignore the doubt Travis had planted in his brain about Jaime's roommate. He'd meant what he'd said when he told Travis he had no right stalking Jaime online. Just because Travis found an online profile that said Jaime was "in a relationship with Aleksandra Lukin" did not mean he was actually in a relationship. Alana was constantly hacking his accounts online and posting about his undying love for Travis, and that would look suspicious if Jaime found it.

Maybe not. She said something about not being around to hear something she felt the need to say in Russian. I have no idea, and I probably don't want to.

Sean shook his head and let his phone fall into his messenger bag as the train stopped. On a Sunday afternoon, most of the passengers took their time, like they were still hungover from the previous night spent in New York before heading back to school. He caught sight of Jaime standing against the wall as he entered the station, and got in a few moments of admiring the way his black tank top showed off the bulk of his arms before Jaime found him in the crowd. His wide smile erased whatever doubts Sean had lingering about Aleksandra. If that hadn't worked, the way Jaime pulled him in by the waistband of his jeans and preceded to kiss him until he couldn't think would have done the trick.

"Hungry?" Jaime asked, moving down to leave a small kiss on his neck.

"Ate lunch on the train."

"My place?"

"Yeah."

Jaime smirked and released him so they could walk to the car. They didn't talk on the ten-minute drive to the apartment, but the way Jaime reached over and moved up his hand up Sean's thigh said more than enough. The way he kept one hand on the wheel and his eyes straight ahead while the fingers of his right hand stroked the inside seam of Sean's jeans had Sean struggling not to slouch in his seat in an attempt to get more contact. When Jaime removed his hand to pull into the parking lot, Sean let himself glare.

"And you've been calling me a tease."

"It's not teasing if I intend to follow through."

Jaime had him pushed up against the door as soon as it closed behind them. He slipped his hands under Sean's T-shirt and pushed it up and off over his head before he dipped back down to mouth at his neck. Jaime was murmuring soft words into his neck, but he gave up concentrating when he realized it was Spanish.

"That is unfairly hot if you're really just reciting your grocery list or something." Sean knew his words came out breathless, but he couldn't be blamed as Jaime fumbled with the button on his jeans, and he chuckled against Sean's neck.

"Maybe I'll translate." Jaime's lips found his again, his teeth nipping at Sean's lower lip before pulling him away from the door and further into the apartment. "Eventually. If I feel like it."

Sean let himself be pushed down on the bed, his flip-flops falling to the floor as Jaime climbed on top of him. Jaime only paused to pull off his own shirt and toss it away before refocusing on Sean's jeans until he had them undone enough to reach inside. Sean bucked against his hand. He scrambled to unbutton Jaime's jeans and push them down. Everything devolved into the slide of skin against skin until he gave in, tightening his own grip as his come left a splatter on Jaime's chest. Jaime pushed into his fist a few more times before collapsing on top of him, his breath hot and fast on Sean's neck. Sean pulled his hand from between them and draped his arm over Jaime's back, enjoying the weight on top of him as his heart rate and breathing settled.

"Worth the train ride?" Jaime raised his head to give him a smirk before pushing off him to move to the edge of the bed. He shucked off his jeans as he stood, leaving them on the floor and walking, naked, to pull a towel off his desk chair to clean himself off before tossing the towel at Sean's chest.

"I'm expecting a round two later where you actually get my jeans off." Sean made a show of tucking himself back into his boxer briefs and started to button his jeans, only to be stopped by Jaime gripping his hand.

"You are not going to lie around in my bed after that with jeans on. That would really ruin all my plans for the day."

Sean laughed, but he lifted his hips to let Jaime pull his jeans off and toss them on the floor.

"You might have to put on clothes to get us food at some point."

"I can warm up last night's dinner. I cooked, and Lexi didn't manage to eat it all. You'll be gone before she realizes it's gone and starts bitching about it."

"Do you not want me to meet her?" Sean asked, although the parts of his brain that were starting to work told him not to.

"What? No." Jaime stretched out next to him on his stomach and propped his head up on Sean's chest. "Well, yes. But only because she will try to intimidate you and insist that you call her Aleksandra, because only my stupidity allows me to get away with saying Lexi. And then she'll try to trick you into some kind of vodka contest that I'm telling you right now you will not win. None of these things fall into my plan today, and if you're too hungover tomorrow, *your* best friend will hate me even more."

"He doesn't hate you." Sean let his fingers drift over Jaime's closed-cropped hair. "He's just overprotective—for mostly no reason. He threatens all Alana's boyfriends when she's obviously ten times scarier than he is, so they all end up thinking he wants to fuck her."

"He doesn't?"

"He knows he's not tough enough for that. He's also eight years older than her, so he thinks she's a kid. He's only four years older than me, and sometimes he forgets I'm not eighteen anymore."

Jaime laughed before turning his head to rest his cheek on Sean's chest as Sean surveyed the room he'd been too preoccupied to notice before. There was an older MacBook sitting on a desk against the wall, and various photographs pinned up around the desk in no apparent order. They weren't the kind he and Travis had up. No random smiling people grouped together casually with their arms draped over each other. These were close-ups of things he couldn't make out. The few with people showed them in private moments he almost felt he shouldn't be watching. He recognized Lupe in one. She was sitting on floor of a studio, bent over in exhaustion with one pointe shoe off and tossed aside.

"She hates that one," Jaime mumbled beside him.

"It's beautiful." He couldn't even pinpoint why.

"Yeah. She just always wants to look perfect all the time."

Sean let his gaze drift from Lupe to a black-and-white of a pretty woman, her hair in loose dark curls as she hung sideways from a pole in short, tight shorts and a bra.

"Should I be worried?" he asked, lifting his hand just enough to point out the picture.

"No. Well, not unless Aleksandra's papa finds it. She dances in clubs sometimes when a friend gets her a gig, but she doesn't strip. Pole's just like a sport to her. I'd argue, but you should see the bruises she comes home from classes with. I took those for a competition she did last month."

"You took all those? I thought you did computer stuff. Like graphics for websites." He was pretty sure he hadn't zoned out of their lunch conversation that much.

"I do. That's where the money is. That's where I can get work that pays enough for rent. But my focus in school is photography. I like it, but after school, that kind of thing will just be a hobby. Lexi thinks I should drop graphic design, but I'd rather do that than end up taking portraits in a department store."

"Maybe you should listen to her."

"I need something more stable—which I realize might not be the thing to say to a dancer, but we can't all be artists." Jaime shrugged and glanced back at the picture before turning back to Sean and climbing farther on top of him. "Not that I'm not flattered you think I'm talented, but I have other talents, and the half-naked girl is not really what's got my attention right now."

SEAN WITHHELD a groan when he opened the door to his apartment and spotted Alana stretched out on the floor, painting her toenails.

"How'd it go? Was it amazing? Are you already naming your hypothetical children I'm not having for you?" Alana asked without looking up or pausing from her work.

"Why are you here?" Sean looked toward the kitchen, but Travis wasn't there, and a glance though the open door to his room didn't give him any hope Travis would appear and declare a ban on discussing Sean's sex life.

"My sister is pissed I accidentally threw out a bag of her clothes. It's not my fault. She put her dirty clothes in a trash bag. Who does that?"

"And Travis left you here?" Sean threw his jacket in his room and went into the kitchen. There was an empty box from a frozen pizza on the counter he was sure Travis hadn't left there. Of course, if Travis stopped stocking the refrigerator with frozen pizzas for her, maybe Alana would stop acting like she lived in their apartment.

"Haven't seen him. One of you left the deadbolt off again. You're going to get robbed. Or stabbed. Or robbed and stabbed." Alana sat back and closed the bottle of nail polish before wandering into Travis's room and coming back with a hoodie. Travis could pretend to kick her out all he wanted. If he wanted Sean to believe he didn't encourage her, he would have to stop letting her take up a quarter of his closet. Sean should find him a girl to date just so he'd have to explain that he'd adopted a really annoying twenty-year-old.

"If anyone breaks in, it's going to be you that stabs and robs them." Sean debated hiding in his room, but she'd just pop his lock with a fork, so he poured a glass of juice and joined her on the couch instead. It was a good thing he'd showered before he'd left Jaime's apartment.

"Because someone has to protect you idiots," Alana said as she lay down on her back with her head in his lap. "So how was it? I can't grill you at class because someone will figure it out, and it will travel back to Lupe eventually."

"It was good." Sean tried to shrug and hold back the smile he knew she'd read too easy, but it was useless when the memory of Jaime's smile and the way it seemed to light up his whole face was so fresh in his mind.

The door opened before Alana could answer, and Travis didn't even react to seeing her on the couch as he picked up her dirty plate from the coffee table and moved it to the sink.

"Sean's all starry-eyed already," Alana called after Travis. He'd object, but it would have been pointless.

CHAPTER 4

SEAN ONLY caught a glimpse of Jaime through the window during class on Tuesday, but he did get a text after that said, *Lupe yelled at me for watching her class. Had to pretend I was watching her at some point.*

Sean figured that was enough encouragement that his text asking if they were hanging out during Lupe's class on Thursday was not a crazy assumption.

Promised Lexi I'd help with a shoot she scheduled at the same time that's also in Chelsea. But you can come with. Might be boring.

Sean didn't hesitate in confirming. It might be boring, but he could meet Aleksandra and make Travis stop giving him pointed looks every time her name came up. Of course, he should have known telling Travis about his plans meant telling Alana, who couldn't just go home after their Thursday ballet class and leave him alone.

"How did I know you were spending half an hour in the dressing room after class so you could look all sexy? Seriously. Everyone is going to know you're dating someone. The girls are already talking about how you smile at all your texts. I tried to tell them Travis finally gave in and decided to be gay for you," Alana said as she walked around the men's dressing room. At least she'd waited until the rest of the guys were gone before coming in this time.

"Why are you here?" Sean threw the rest of his things in his bag. Jaime would be around soon. He'd need to wait until Lupe and Michael were occupied to meet him at his car, but he also didn't want to take too long when Aleksandra would be waiting on him also.

Alana shrugged and didn't spout off a quick answer. That was never a good sign.

"Okay, really, why are you here?" Sean asked again, this time actually stopping what he was doing to look at her.

"My mom has a date. She's cooking him dinner at the house." Alana scrunched up her nose. "She didn't tell me until this morning."

"And Travis actually has his own date at the apartment because he knew I'd be gone tonight," Sean finished for her.

"Don't tell him. You know he works too hard. He hasn't had a girlfriend since before the accident." Alana shrugged. "Plus the small practice room is empty in a couple hours. I need to work on that combination for Steph's piece anyway. If I have to overhear Amy say I don't have enough classical training to do it one more time, she might have to accidentally fall down the stairs."

"So you're going to sit around for two hours?" Sean was going to hate himself for it later and he knew it, but he picked up his phone to text Jaime as Alana shrugged and laid down on one of the long benches.

Is it okay if Alana comes with? If not, it's okay. But she's kind of stranded with nothing to do for 2 hours. I feel bad even if she will make me regret it if I invite her.

Jaime's reply was fast enough that Sean hoped he was already parked.

Why would you regret it?

She will probably tell you embarrassing things about me on purpose.

She is officially invited.

"You want to come with me?" Sean asked. She was still going to mortify him, but it was worth it to get the genuine small smile she didn't usually let out.

"Thanks." Alana sat up and Sean turned away to give his hair a final check in one of the mirrors while she slid back on the mask of sarcasm they were both more used to. "Seriously. Your hair is not that long. You only have so many options, but you spend more time on it than I do."

Jaime was already out of the car when Sean and Alana turned the corner. His trunk was open, and the brunette Sean recognized from the picture was unloading equipment and handing it to him. Sean didn't have time to try and figure out how to get around the bulk in Jaime's arms for a greeting kiss before she was pushing a bag at him.

"Jaime probably left out the part where you both have to carry all my stuff. He's using you to not have to carry it all himself." Aleksandra pulled a tripod out of the trunk and handed it to him before he could respond. "If that bothers you, blame him for going on about how you're a dancer and you have all these muscles."

"It's no problem." Sean glanced at Jaime, who tried to manage a shrug under his own load as Aleksandra closed the trunk and walked around them to lead the way.

"I can take something." Alana offered Jaime, whose load seemed more awkward than Sean's own.

"Oh, don't let him," Aleksandra interrupted. "He needs the workout to keep up with your boy if he's going to kick me out of the apartment for hours on the weekend."

"See! Other people talk to their friends." Alana glared at Sean before moving around him to walk in front with Aleksandra. "Seriously. Help. We can't get details out of him. If I hadn't seen Jaime with my own eyes, I wouldn't even know what he looked like."

"I was hoping Alana would cancel out Lexi. They're just going to multiply each other, aren't they?" Jaime whispered.

"Probably."

"THIS IS awesome. This is ten times cooler than go-go dancing in stupid cages," Alana whispered. She was sitting next to Sean on the floor in the corner of the studio where Aleksandra was taking pictures of various dancers. The studio wasn't too different from the one where they'd had class earlier. Mirrors lined every wall, but instead of barres bracketed to the walls, six shiny metal poles stretched from floor to ceiling around the room.

"Which is already something Travis does not want you doing for extra money," Sean pointed out. Travis was going to kill him when he found out Sean had taken Alana to a pole-dancing studio. "And I'm pretty sure his argument that you can't do it because you might get injured and end your career actually applies in this case."

"Hey." Jaime sat down next to him close enough that their shoulders pressed together. "She's good without me until she finishes the group shots. Sorry that she's extra intense today. I should have remembered not to introduce her to people when she's working. Bored yet?"

"Bored?" Sean watched as a dancer climbed up a pole and flipped upside down into a pose. "I'm not sure how you were impressed with us. We can do that, but not while hanging upside down."

Jaime laughed and gestured around the room of women with his hand.

"Not exactly my type. But if you want to try and get up there, I'm sure Lexi would help you for me when she's done, if there's time."

"I'll do it," Alana said.

"Travis would kill me for the injury risk first, and then he'd kill me again for letting you do it." Sean turned to Jaime. "Travis doesn't actually hate you. Let her get on a pole, and he will hate us both."

"Seriously? I think she scares me more than him," Jaime said as he took in Alana's glare.

"It's cute how you think it's about letting me do anything. You know I can just come here and take classes if I want. My contract does not actually ban outside classes," Alana answered.

"It would be like encouraging Lupe to do it," Sean said. Jaime cringed.

"Understood. Not letting either of you pole dance." Jaime ignored Alana's groan and leaned closer to whisper, "But if you want, I could set something up later for you. She has her own pole at the apartment."

Sean couldn't help letting a shiver go through him as Jaime grazed the back of his hand down Sean's arm. Jaime leaned in to brush their lips together for just a moment before Aleksandra motioned for him.

"Fine. Because you are cute, and I don't actually want Travis to kill your boyfriend, I will wait and do this behind your backs. I do so much for you," Alana said as soon as Jaime was out of earshot.

Jaime didn't make it back to them until he was finished with his own shots and Aleksandra was working with the last remaining dancer. Jaime had packed up the equipment they were finished using, and sat down next to Sean with one of the digital cameras. It was fancier than anything Sean had used, but he took most of his pictures with his phone. Jaime tilted the camera so Sean could see one of the pictures on the small screen as Aleksandra finished her work and walked back to them.

"His are just as good as mine. I keep telling him to stop wasting all his time doing stupid corporate website graphics, but he does not listen," Aleksandra said, tilting the camera to look at few herself. "*Takoy glupynik.*"

"Was that offensive?" Sean looked from Aleksandra to Jaime.

"Probably. Dirty generally has a different tone," Jaime said as he started to get up and gather the equipment together.

"Well, I don't know if I can recognize how good you are. I'm not a photographer. But if you're good, and you love it, I think you should go for it. I couldn't stop dancing because it wasn't practical."

"It's different." Jaime shook his head and handed Sean an assortment of equipment.

"Because you are too scared of failure," Aleksandra said, picking up the same bag she'd carried before and turning to face Sean. "Teach him that passion is worth something, and maybe you will actually stay."

SEAN SQUINTED at the dim light as he woke up and adjusted to his surroundings. He turned to his right side to check the time before he remembered he wasn't home, and Jaime kept his alarm clock turned to the wall where the light wouldn't bother him.

"Hey. Sorry. Did I wake you up?" Jaime asked as he swiveled his desk chair around to face the bed. Only his desk lamp was on to supplement the glow from his computer, where he had one of the pictures from Thursday's shoot pulled up.

"Maybe. Time?" Sean stretched and sat up.

"Three-thirty. Sorry. I couldn't sleep, and I need to get these retouched and sent back early. Lexi showed them to the studio with some of hers, and they picked mine for the ads they're putting out."

"Is she mad?" Sean asked. The last he'd heard, it was her job she'd just conned Jaime into helping with.

"No." Jaime chuckled and shook his head. "She's using it as an argument that I shouldn't take the web design job I already have lined up after graduation. She's trying to convince me that photography is practical if I apply to ad agencies or magazines or something. It's her new angle."

"But you don't agree?" Sean inched to the edge of the bed, taking the blankets with him.

"Breaking into magazines and ad agencies means interning. Usually for credit and not money. The internship I did last summer for the web design company actually paid enough that I could fill out the rest of the rent bartending on weekends. Magazine internships are for the kids whose parents can pay their rent while they work for free."

"But Lupe's managing hers. We're not exactly paying her." He was pretty sure they weren't—though Travis might have tried if she'd started to turn it down.

"I'm helping her with food money." Jaime shook his head when Sean opened his mouth to answer. "I shouldn't have told you that. She doesn't want you guys to know."

"Why?" Sean was sure if Travis knew he'd probably feed her as often as he did Alana.

"She wants him to offer her a spot in the company because he wants her, not because if she doesn't get something from a company right after she graduates, she'll have to go back home. But she's willing to hope and risk it. I can't do that. I can't start focusing on some hope I'll get a job in an industry I haven't interned for, and then go home if I fail."

"If I ask why again, are you going get annoyed with me? Because there isn't another train back to New York until tomorrow, and I'm kind of afraid of what Aleksandra will do to me if I'm on the couch." Sean added the small smile that could usually keep Alana from sighing and declaring him a total lost cause to whatever she thought he was wrong about.

"No. Maybe annoyed, but I'm too selfish to send you to the couch, and if I did and you explained why, she'd just bring you to her side even more. Not a risk worth taking. I'm already annoyed she's clearly recruited you to this argument with one conversation." Jaime turned back to the computer and started saving the files he had open. For a minute, Sean wondered if he was waiting for Sean to actually come out and ask, but when Sean opted to stay silent, Jaime seemed to take that as enough of a prompt.

"I'm out here. Even with Lupe here, I only see her a few times a week. If she signs with the company and moves to the city, it's still a big enough city, or if it seems not to be, there are a lot of web design and development jobs in California. I can get something with it, I'm sure. I do graphics at school, but I've done programming at work and on my own. If I go home, out isn't an option. It's just not. As long as I'm a thousand miles away, it's easy to separate."

"You're never planning to tell them?" Sean forced himself not to choke on the words as he tried to ignore the weight on his chest that shouldn't be there if Jaime was throwing out the option to move to California without even thinking about him.

"There's not really a point. I know how it would go, so why bother? We're Catholic. Eventually, I might have to say I broke up with Lexi or something, but they'll get over that." Jaime hit the button to turn off his monitor and turned around to face him. "As long as I have a job and I'm doing what I'm supposed to, they don't ask about anything else. I only see them once or twice a year."

"Don't you want to tell them the truth?"

"It's not just about what I want, Sean. My mom worked hard so I can be here, so I could even go to college, because she never could. The church helped her do that. It would kill her if I just left it."

"You don't have to pick. There are out Catholics. People change."

"Your people change. Not my people," Jaime said. "Drop it, okay? It doesn't matter if they know."

Sean swallowed his instinct to ask how it could not matter forever, and moved up the bed as Jaime lay back down next to him.

SUN WAS already streaming through the window when Sean stretched and rolled over to reach the other side of the bed to find it empty. As he woke up, he could hear voices in the kitchen but couldn't make out any words. His clothes were still on the floor were they had fallen as Jaime stripped him on the way to the bed, but his phone had been left for him on the nightstand. He had one message from Alana from late the night before.

I talked Travis into making steaks tomorrow night. Will you be home by 7 or should I pretend I need to eat later so he doesn't say it's Jaime's job to feed you if he keeps you all day?

He sent off a text that he'd be home by five before sitting up in the bed. He should probably go out there. Maybe Jaime had gotten up because he was hungry or bored, and if he'd tried to wake Sean up, that probably hadn't worked well. He knew halfhearted attempts to wake him up were usually so unsuccessful that he didn't even remember them, and the last time he'd stayed over, Jaime had needed to get up early for a meeting, so Sean had known in advance he'd wake up alone. This time, he'd hoped for a lazy morning in bed without even realizing it. Maybe Jaime was just a morning person. He'd never actually known a morning person before. Even Travis slept until nine on Sunday mornings unless he had a reason not to. It was only ten now. He would have rolled over and gone back to sleep if Jaime had still been asleep next to him. Once, Travis had dated a girl who got up every morning at eight and ran a mile. What if Jaime was like that?

Or maybe he'd decided to get up because lying in bed with Sean in the morning without sex wasn't something he was interested in. Maybe a few weeks into dating was too early for Sean to sleep over a second time. It wouldn't be the first time he'd thought a guy wanted him around more than he really did, but Jaime couldn't have thought he'd have enough time to go home when he'd invited Sean to come over the night before.

The door crept open and Jaime smiled when he saw Sean was up.

"Hey." Jaime closed the door behind him and walked to the bed. "I thought you were going to sleep through breakfast."

"Breakfast?" Sean was more of a brunch person. Sometimes when he had to get up early for classes, Travis would make him eat a bagel.

"Are you on some weird dancer diet that doesn't let you eat breakfast?" Jaime climbed on the bed and crawled over Sean so he was pressing Sean down on his back as Jaime nipped at his neck. "Because I was thinking you'd need the energy, and I don't have any weird diet shakes or anything."

"I usually sleep through it," Sean mumbled as Jaime pressed a soft kiss to the base of his neck.

"Well, if you want something since you woke up, it's ready." Jaime pulled back, smirking at Sean's soft whine of protest. "I'm not going to make you get up before you want to on your day off, but I'm warning you that there's a limit on how long Lexi will save you some."

With that, Jaime left him, closing the door behind him. Part of Sean wanted to sleep for another hour. He couldn't relax with the warmth that came over him as he realized no guy had ever cooked him breakfast. Maybe he had been missing out by not dating morning people. No, he was not going to get up early all the time, but Jaime had no way of knowing he usually slept until eleven on Sundays. What mattered was that he'd made breakfast the first morning they really had to spend together.

Jaime was at the stove when Sean came out to the kitchen wearing the same clothes he'd had on the night before. He'd assumed he was spending the night, but bringing extra clothes seemed like too much. He'd tried to make something of his hair in the small mirror in Jaime's room before deciding he'd just have to face Aleksandra on the way to the bathroom.

"He wakes." Aleksandra was sitting at the table with one leg curled under her on the small padded folding chair. Sean couldn't imagine it was comfortable, but she seemed to think so. Her hair was in messy dark waves around her shoulders, and she was still dressed in a tank top and pajama pants Sean assumed she'd slept in.

"Yeah. Good morning?" Sean glanced behind Aleksandra toward the bathroom, and she laughed as she waved him away.

"Go ahead. I'm not as uncivilized as this one makes me out to be. I'll leave you something to eat."

"Yeah. She'll just eat my food instead," Jaime said as Sean closed the door to the bathroom and surveyed his options. Jaime's hair was trimmed so close to his head that any hair products had to be Aleksandra's, and he should probably not steal her products without asking. Instead, he'd just have to hope water would make whatever gel was left in his hair from the day before hold some kind of a decent shape. He splashed his face with water and gave up hope there was a moisturizer he could use without getting caught. If his skin felt dry later, he'd just do a mask. It was always worth doing with Alana anyway, because Travis hated looking at them.

"Do you like breakfast burritos?" Jaime asked when he came back in the kitchen. "If you don't, there's also bacon because Lexi demanded some, or you could have eggs without all the fun stuff if you wanted. There's also cereal, because Lexi has to eat something when I'm not home."

"A breakfast burrito's good."

"Usually he makes them spicier, but he was afraid you couldn't handle it, so they're not as good," Aleksandra said as she took another bite of her own.

"They're just as good." Jaime set a plate in front of him. There was already orange juice on the table, so Sean shook his head at the offer of coffee.

"You don't drink coffee?" Aleksandra stared at him like he'd just told her he murdered small children.

"Sometimes, if I didn't sleep well, but not all the time. It makes me jittery."

"And you slept really well last night, I'm sure." Aleksandra smirked as she picked up her own mug of coffee and sat back to pretzel herself in the chair.

CHAPTER 5

SEAN WAS loitering in the dressing room on Thursday almost three weeks later when Alana sauntered in after everyone else had left. It was the one day a week Jaime was in the city, and Sean's schedule was easy enough that he wasn't useless. The short time span meant they had to spend the time just hanging out and talking instead of hooking up. The previous week Alana had figured out how much he was looking forward to it and spent the entire day teasing him for being more excited about getting to know Jaime than having a sex marathon on the weekend.

"Why are you pouty? Teasing you for being excited for your weekly sexless date night is not fun if you are not actually excited for it." Alana wiped her hand over the nearest bench before deciding it was clean enough to lie down on her back. "Don't worry. I'm not invading again. I wish I was. Travis is coming back to help me work on Steph's piece. You might need to come back after the date to carry me home, though."

"Tell Travis if he kills you, it's his job to carry you home," Sean answered.

"I did notice you ignored the other question. Why are you pouty? Did he cancel? Does he have something else to do and he said you can't come with? Did he give you herpes?"

"What?" Sean stopped tossing stuff in his bag to look at her.

"You weren't reacting to anything. I took a guess."

"And you guessed herpes?"

"So it's not herpes, then?" Alana asked, as though she actually deserved an answer. "Or it is herpes? Because Travis is really going to freak out if Jaime gave you herpes. Or did some other guy call and say he might have given you herpes, and now you have to tell Jaime the herpes is your fault?"

"No. What is wrong with you? No one gave anyone else herpes!" This sentence, of course, would be Travis's cue to show up.

"Is there a story here I should be concerned about?" he asked.

"No. Unless something personal has made your crazy adoptive daughter think about herpes too much." Sean would have felt bad about the look Alana got from Travis if she hadn't deserved it.

"What? I don't have herpes!" Alana cast him a glare before turning back to Travis. "Travis, I swear I did not do anything to get herpes. Sean is being pouty about his date. I merely guessed that maybe it was because he had herpes."

Travis looked back at her for a moment before sighing and raising his gaze to the ceiling. His lips moved in a silent count to ten before he looked back down and ignored Alana to look at Sean.

"Right. So now that we've cleared that up, is there an actual problem here?"

"Not really." Sean glanced at his phone. He still had at least a few minutes before Jaime would text him and save him from this mess.

"Not really, or just no, there is not a problem, and Alana just wanted an excuse to scare the shit out of me?" Travis's face was already shifting from the exhausted look Alana often inspired in him to the concerned one that made Sean want to hide from him.

"Not really, as in I'm making up a problem in my head that is not really a problem or anything I should be upset about, so you can drop the mother hen act before you start." Sean sighed and rolled his eyes when Travis's expression didn't relax. "Really. It's stupid, and I haven't mentioned it to him at all. If you go after him, he will just be confused and possibly ask me why I didn't just ask him myself, so please refrain from making me look stupid."

"In that case, this would be easier and more convincing if you'd tell me exactly what the issue is so I can just not worry about it, and

Alana can stop acting like I don't know she's trying to shorten her rehearsal by getting you to drag out this conversation."

Sean considered avoiding the question again, but that would just help Alana, and Travis would still harass him when he got home.

"He hasn't said if he's coming to opening night. But it's not a big deal if he does, and he probably will anyway because Lupe is supposed to come. He's not suddenly going to decide she can come here even later at night by herself."

"But you're not sure if he's going to drop her off or stay and watch you dance—which he really should do, considering that he's been dating you for almost two months," Travis finished for him, and then ran his hand over his face when Sean didn't deny it. "I think you know the solution is to just ask him, but considering I can't seem to keep him from smudging up the window when he spies on you during every rehearsal, if he passes on the real thing, you should probably worry about his fixation with breathing all over clean glass. Tell him he owes me some Windex. I don't even let mothers hover like that over my level-two class."

"I will make sure to bring that up." Sean couldn't help laughing.

"But you knew he'd never be able to go as your boyfriend. He'll have to pretend he's there for Lupe at the cast party." Travis shifted back to his worried gaze. "Is that going to be enough for you?"

"I know that. I'll know why he's there. That's what matters."

Travis didn't look like he believed it, but Sean's vibrating phone saved him anyway.

Back seat of my car?

Sean laughed and ignored the eye rolls he was sure Travis and Alana were sharing over his reaction to the text in favor of typing back. *Still not happening.*

Fine. Then I hope you have energy to walk around. I have spent too much of my day sitting in this fucking car.

"Talk to him," Travis called after him. Sean held up a hand to flip him off instead of answering as he made his way out of the dressing room.

"Hey." Jaime didn't move from his position leaning against the car to meet him, but as soon as Sean was close enough, he pulled Sean close. Jaime skipped a normal greeting kiss in favor of turning his head to the side to mouth up Sean's neck from his collarbone until he could nibble on the lobe of Sean's ear.

"Car is still an option, *querido*." Jaime's breath was hot in his ear, and he slipped his thumb under Sean's shirt to stroke the bare skin of his hip. It was almost enough for Sean to forget he was above hooking up in the back seat of an old Camaro.

"The Spanish is cheating. I can never even remember what you're saying so I can look it up later." Sean knew his voice was rough as Jaime grazed his teeth down Sean's neck.

"*Tu me vuelves loco.*" Jaime's tongue flicked his ear as he finished.

"Did you just call me crazy? I know *loco* is crazy. Are you actually insulting me while trying to get in my pants?"

Jaime sighed and let his forehead drop onto the crook of Sean's neck with a short laugh.

"I didn't call you crazy, but the statement is really accurate now." Jaime groaned as Sean pulled away.

"Well, you're crazy if you think I'm ever hooking up in the backseat of your car," Sean said as he stepped back. He let his hand skim down Jaime's arm until he reached his hand to pull him away from the car. "You wanted to walk."

"I wanted to blow you. Walking was very much a second-choice activity." Jaime tried to pull him back, but Sean pulled harder, dragging Jaime along until he gave up and relaxed into an easy stride next to him.

"Should I worry about your one-track mind?" Sean went for light, but had to force himself to look ahead and not study Jaime's face for a reaction.

"You should take the compliment." Jaime tugged his hand to lead him down around the next corner before letting go and shoving his hands in the pockets of his black leather jacket. The fall hadn't really shifted to cold yet, but Sean told himself the sun was setting, and it was getting there as he copied the action so he didn't feel like his hand was dangling empty.

"Still driving next week?" Sean asked. It wasn't exactly what he wanted to ask, but it was something. They had two dress rehearsals at night that Lupe was supposed to watch, and Sean would be dancing through most of them, but he couldn't help wanting Jaime there.

"Monday and Thursday, but I have class Wednesday night, so Lexi's driving then. Lupe will probably even let her stay because she's cooler than me. So if you mess up, I'll hear about it. She'll probably sneak in a camera and take a picture if you fall." Jaime laughed at Sean's glare. "Go ahead. You tell her she has to follow the rules."

"Right. I have to be perfect on Wednesday."

"Exactly." Jaime smiled and stepped closer to bump his shoulder.

"And Friday?" Sean asked, unable to lift his eyes from where his feet hit the dirty sidewalk with each stride.

"On Friday, I'm bringing Lexi with me so Lupe will let me stay for the whole thing. She might even let me follow Lexi into the cast party after—during which she is not allowed to drink, by the way."

"Seriously?" Sean laughed, letting the smile that had been growing stay. "Travis even lets Alana drink at cast parties. He doesn't know she refills her one glass of champagne little by little while he's not looking, but he lets her have it."

"You haven't told him?"

"Not getting in the middle of that." Sean shook his head. "But I make no promises she won't teach that trick to Lupe."

"Lupe can drink in front of me next year when she's legal. I don't care how much bitching I have to hear about it on Friday." Jaime groaned and lifted one of his hands out of his pocket to rub over his short hair. "And there will be bitching if Alana gets to drink."

"She's going to hate it when Travis ends up even more overprotective than you."

"She idolizes him. Can you just get him to tell her drinking is bad? Maybe throw in that sex and drugs will ruin her career?"

"I'm not sure if I'm relieved that you'll clearly get along with him when he decides to give you a chance, or if I'm terrified Alana's been right all along." Sean figured he should be more worried about how much shit Alana was going to give him if she decided he'd just found a gay version of Travis.

"Right about what?" Jaime stopped at a bench and sat down, leaving space for Sean to sit next to him.

"Nothing." Sean sat closer than he felt he should, but it still wasn't as close as he wanted. Jaime didn't move away, but he didn't close the space either. If he didn't want to move closer, he probably wasn't ready to hear Alana's crazy theories about him and Travis. "So I'll see you there?"

"Yeah. I mean, we can't—"

"I know," Sean said before he could finish. "It's okay. But you'll be there."

"Well, yeah." Jaime turned his head to the side and looked at him, searching his face like he wasn't sure what he was even looking for.

"Good. That's good." Sean found himself struggling to think up any other topic before a silence could set in. "That presentation you were working on, how'd it turn out?"

Jaime hesitated like he knew there was something he'd missed, but instead of probing, he leaned back on the bench again and launched into his answer.

*C*HAPTER 6

"SHE'S NOT even late," Sean pointed out when Travis looked at his watch for the second time. He turned away from Travis to face the barre. Maybe if he focused enough on the warm-up, Travis would only punish Alana for her lateness.

"She'll be late in ten minutes—which will make her ten minutes late unless she did her warm-up on the way."

Sean didn't have to look to know Travis was glaring at the door like it would make Alana walk through it. When Travis walked to him to correct his form a minute later, he knew better than to argue that Travis hadn't actually changed the position of his leg at all. When the door creaked open a few minutes later, Travis didn't turn around.

"You're late. I'm not letting you start until you're warmed up, so you're late."

Alana didn't answer. Instead, she took a spot on a barre across the room instead of next to him, even though they were the only dancers in the room. Sean hazarded a look over his shoulder, but couldn't catch her eye in the mirror at all. When she still hadn't filled the space with her normal chatter two minutes before rehearsal, Travis sighed.

"I'm going to regret this, and I know it, but what's wrong? You have two minutes."

Alana stepped away from the barre and walked to them, her pointe shoes clunking on the floor. She looked at Travis first, and then let her eyes flick to Sean for a second before looking at the floor. He could see Travis shift from annoyed to worried just before she steeled herself and looked up as she settled her hands on her hips.

"This is probably going to make us late. We'll be dealing with it more than two minutes, and we won't be able to make it up, because we should really not run late today—which is why I figured I'd try to make it through rehearsal and then try to make Sean take me home for some reason, but I just can't. I can't go through this whole rehearsal like nothing is wrong."

"The show opens next week. This rehearsal is not getting cut short. The interns can sit and watch if they need to."

"Or you could cancel them? Maybe call Lupe right now?" Alana suggested, as if Travis had ever canceled a rehearsal in his entire career.

"Not a chance." Travis shook his head. "Just get out with it. We'll talk about whatever it is, and then rehearsal is starting no matter what it is."

"Okay, okay, but you have to let me get through the whole thing. Because I'm going to say the first part, and you're going to want to yell at me, so clearly there is a second part that is more important, if I'm telling you the part that's going to make you yell at me. Otherwise I would not just tell on myself when I know you're going to actually come back and remember to be mad at me for it after all the other shit is dealt with." Alana stood with her hands on her hips while she waited for Travis to answer.

Travis pinched the bridge of his nose as he nodded and waved his hand for her to move on with it.

"So, Shalonda called me last night and said a lot of the dancers called in, and yes, I know, I know, you hate when I take work go-go dancing, but Mom's been taking so many shifts to cover Diana's tuition, and it's not like they can even really touch me, because I always just dance in the cages, and you know I'm not going to really get injured, and no, I'm not letting you pay me not to do it."

"Is this the part I'm supposed to be mad about later?" Travis said through his teeth. "Because it's going to happen, but if there's more, you should move on."

"Right. So, you know I don't do it that often because it's really not worth pissing you off if you find out, so I don't know most of the girls, and I usually go home before the pole dancers because they bring them on later, and if I take the late-night shift, I'm exhausted in the morning."

"Aleksandra was dancing?" Sean filled in for her. "That's not news. She doesn't do it all the time either, but she probably got called like you did."

"I know, and I was just going to say hi later. And okay, I was also going to beg her not to tell Jaime or Sean." Alana sighed and took a deep breath. "But then I realized Jaime was there. With a guy."

"He can have friends," Sean interrupted, but he knew on some level there was more.

"That he makes out with on the dance floor? Because that doesn't seem like an arrangement you'd like or agree to. I'm sorry. I couldn't just not tell you. I'm sorry."

Out of the corner of his eye, he could see Alana looking to Travis for help as he backed away from them.

"He never said." Sean shook his head and tried to blink away the tears starting to collect in his eyes. "I mean, we haven't talked about it. He never said there wasn't anyone else or that it was just me."

"But you thought there wasn't," Travis said as he moved toward Sean again.

"It's stupid," Sean mumbled as he felt Travis's hand on his shoulder. The worst part was that Travis wasn't even surprised, because it wasn't the first time he'd watched Sean build something up in his head that ended up not being half as real as he wanted it to be.

"Hey, no. It's not stupid. He's a fucking moron. That's what it is," Travis said with a slight growl in his voice that Sean didn't even have the drive to tell him to drop. Travis tugged at his shoulder, and Sean gave in to the urge to slump against him and then bury his face in Travis's chest to hide the tears sliding down his face. Travis's arms came up around him. He was silent and still, with one hand firm on Sean's back and the other holding the back of Sean's head as Sean tried to settle himself with deep breaths.

"Check the hall," Travis said over him when he'd finally calmed enough to breathe normally.

"It's empty. Just us," Alana answered.

"You're going to finish warming up. We're going to go clean Sean up, and then we're starting. Five minutes. I mean it. Five minutes."

Travis steered him down the deserted hall with an arm around his shoulders. Travis scheduled rehearsals on Saturday mornings so no one would see too much of his new choreography before opening night, and Sean was never going to hate him for it again. Travis left him slumped on a bench in the dressing room while he disappeared for a few seconds and came back with a damp paper towel and wad of toilet paper. He sighed and squatted on the floor in front of Sean.

"If you make me do this for you, I'm going to be even more worried, I'm going to make rehearsal even longer, and I'm going to make Alana take you home afterward so I can go buy a shovel."

Sean rolled his eyes, but he took the tissue and blew his nose before taking the towel and wiping the tear tracks from his face.

"Okay. We're going back, and we're finishing rehearsal. If you manage to not completely suck, I will maybe end the rehearsal on time," Travis said as he gripped Sean's arm and pulled him off the bench.

"I hate you," Sean mumbled, but there was no heat in it.

Alana stepped away from the barre when they entered and met them in the middle of the floor. Travis might have seen him make too much of almost every guy he'd slept with since they met, but it wasn't like he'd ever invited Alana over for the show.

"It's okay. You didn't do anything," Sean said before she could apologize again. He pulled her into a quick hug as Travis spoke over his head.

"Except that stuff she did do that we're having a talk about when it doesn't run even further into our rehearsal."

"This is going to suck so much." Alana groaned and pulled away from him so they could get to their starting positions. She wasn't wrong. Sean knew on some level that Travis was torturing him to keep his mind off everything else, but when Travis called an end to rehearsal, he still fell to the floor without even looking at the time.

"Stretch out," Travis said as he pulled Alana to her feet next to him. She tossed a panicked look over at Sean but Travis just handed her something from his bag, and whatever he said was not long enough for a talk about her foray back to the club.

"Come on," Alana said when she got back to him. "Move before he changes his mind and remembers how mad he is at me."

Sean started to protest that he needed to shower when he realized Lupe and Michael hadn't shown up at the door. A glance at the clock told him hell had actually frozen over. Travis had ended rehearsal a full ten minutes early.

"I know. And he gave me cab money because he loves you, but it's going to be pointless if we don't go. Unless you want to actually confront him, but then Travis might decide we can rehearse for ten more minutes."

"I thought you weren't going to send Alana home with me," Sean said as Alana pulled him up and handed him his things.

"I never said that—or promised not to buy the shovel. But I have to stay. If I cancel...." Travis didn't finish the sentence, but he didn't have to. Travis never canceled any rehearsals. If he did, the whole company would want to know why.

Sean nodded and followed Alana out of the room and down the stairs. At least he could appreciate her ability to hail a cab in ten seconds at any given moment.

"Are you actually under orders to follow me into the apartment?"

"I'm not doing anything to make him any madder at me, so you're pretty much stuck with me," Alana answered as she leaned against him in the back of the cab. She was quiet for the ride and the walk to the apartment, but she called out as he moved to the bathroom to shower.

"Sean? Should I just not have said anything?"

"No." Sean sighed and leaned against the doorframe. "It's better that I know sooner than later."

"Okay." Alana let him close the bathroom door before calling in, "Travis said not to let you shower longer than twenty minutes. Otherwise, I have permission to go in and drag you out in case you're crying."

"I hate you both," Sean called back.

Sean had three texts from Jaime ten minutes apart and a missed call when he got out of the shower and dug his phone out of his dance bag.

Outside in the usual spot.

We had plans, right?

Ok. Did I miss something? If I'd known I was getting stood up, I would have brought reading for class to kill time.

"Don't call him," Alana said. She was leaning against the door to his bedroom in sweats and a T-shirt. She'd taken her own shower in only five minutes.

"I stood him up, and he doesn't know why." Sean scrolled back through the last few weeks of text history filled with casual comments, plans to meet up, and more than a few sexts. There was nothing he really should have gotten feelings from. "He never told me he wasn't seeing anyone else."

"You are the most transparent person I've ever met. If he didn't know how you felt, he didn't want to know." Alana lay down on the bed next to him and turned on her side to face him. "Also, if I let you call him, Travis will be mad at me. More mad at me. If I have to guilt you into not calling him by reminding you that I told on myself for your sake, I am not above that."

Sean didn't answer as he scrolled through his texts again.

"Come on. Leave it for now." Alana eased the phone out of his hand and set it on the table by his bed. "I will even watch shitty Lifetime TV with you. We'll make Travis cook us dinner when he gets home. I'll text him."

"Jaime can cook. He makes breakfast when I stay over." Maybe because he couldn't cook, Sean had made something out of that. He had wanted to ignore the evidence that Jaime made breakfast every day, whether he was there or not.

"I'm sure Travis can beat him in grilled cheese skills. He'll throw in some bacon. You can have bacon. You have earned bacon." Alana flipped the remote to some kind of reality show and picked up her phone to text Travis before settling against Sean.

He managed to pretend to pay attention to the show Alana had put on, but he still jumped when his phone vibrated forty minutes later.

"Maybe it's Travis," Sean said when Alana stopped him from reaching for it.

"I told Travis to text me so you wouldn't have to pick up your phone."

"What if it's my mom?" Sean knew his mom would be more likely to call, but it wasn't like Jaime was the only person to ever text him.

"It's not your mom, but if you're going to read it, I might as well be here to keep you from being stupid about it." Alana sighed and picked up the phone herself to hand it to him.

Lupe said you were already gone and you left rehearsal early. Are you ok? Did you get hurt? Can you just tell me if you're ok so I can be pissed off at you instead of worried?

"I have to answer him. It's not fair." Sean tilted the phone so Alana could see the text.

"I can answer him for you," Alana suggested.

Sean ignored her suggestion. Anything she'd text would involve some kind of graphic removal of organs if she was in the mood to be nice. It took typing and deleting three drafts before he gave up and sent something simple.

I'm ok.

Lupe is bitching at me for texting and driving even though we're not moving in this traffic, but that's a shit answer. If you want to give me a better one when I get home, let me know.

"He has no right," Alana said after reading over his shoulder.

"He kind of does, if you want to get technical about it. He didn't do anything wrong because he never said he wasn't seeing anyone else, and I stood him up with no explanation."

"Technicalities are fucking nothing. But if you want to argue with me, I'm just going to appeal to the part of you that doesn't want him to crash his car and die and point out that you really can't keep texting him while he's driving. Because Lupe and Michael might die too, and they really don't deserve that."

Sean let his phone fall back to the bed and shifted to turn away from her. Jaime was right. He knew in his head that he was being an ass, but if he called Jaime, it wasn't really going to get any better.

"I have to face him eventually." Sean mumbled it, but Alana answered anyway.

"The offer still stands to have me tell him off without you ever having to talk to him again."

Sean nodded and let himself zone out as she rubbed his back.

When he woke an hour later, he didn't remember falling asleep, but Alana wasn't with him in the bed anymore. He heard movement in the kitchen and turned to face the door when it creaked open.

"There's food," Travis said. "Eat regular meals, and I'll leave you alone until Monday."

Sean glanced at the table by his bed, but his phone wasn't there.

"It's in the living room. We didn't want it to wake you up, but he called," Travis said as he leaned against the doorframe. Sean tried to ignore the jump in his chest that came from knowing Jaime had at least called, but even Travis probably read it on his face.

"I need to call him back." Sean waited for Travis to argue, but he nodded instead.

"You should wake up and eat first."

"You're not going to argue?"

"I'm going to argue if you call him and say everything is fine. Otherwise, I agree you should call him and tell him how he fucked up and dump his sorry ass." Travis shrugged. "You sulk longer if you don't have closure."

"I hate you."

"Get up. There's sandwiches and soup." Travis turned to leave, and then seemed to think better of it and turned back. "Do you want me to send Alana home?"

Sean shook his head as he got off the bed. At least she'd be annoying enough to distract him, plus she'd override Travis's TV choices and let Sean watch as much shitty TV as he wanted.

Travis gave up his phone after he'd eaten. There was one missed call, but no voice mail because Jaime didn't know Sean wanted to be with him, but he knew Sean hated checking his voice mail. There was one last text instead.

That was my last call until you feel like calling me. I'm just going to assume I should drop Lupe off at rehearsal Monday and go study somewhere else.

Sean stared at his phone for a minute before getting up and going to his room. Alana got up, but Sean assumed Travis stopped her from following because no one kept him from closing the door. He hit the button to call back as he lay on his back on the bed.

"I didn't think you'd call." Jaime skipped the hello. He always did. He said if someone was calling him, saying hello was a waste of time and minutes because they wouldn't call him if they didn't want to talk to him.

"Sorry. I should have texted and canceled."

"That would have been better." Jaime's sigh into the phone was harsh. "Sean, what's going on?"

Sean tried to find the right words, but ended up taking so long to answer that Jaime spoke again.

"Hey. I'm really having a hard time believing that you're okay right now. Lupe said Travis was being weird. Is he okay? She thinks I'm too interested in her life now. Do you want me to come over?"

"No." Sean closed his eyes to try and block the tears and focus. "Fuck. Why are you acting like you care?"

"I'm sorry. Am I not supposed to care about my friends?"

"Friends? We're fucking every weekend, and we're *friends*? That's what you do with your friends? Alana saw you making out with another one of your friends last night. I'm sorry. I just misunderstood, since I don't fuck Travis or Alana."

Jaime didn't answer right away, and Sean was sure he could hear the sob Sean let slip.

"Sean. Fuck. Sean, I'm sorry." Jaime took a deep breath, and Sean knew on some level that he wasn't going to say what Sean wanted. "Sean, I didn't know you thought we were more. That's just not what I'm looking for. I—"

"If you're going to say you're not that into me or that it's not me, it's you, can you just stop?" Sean interrupted. "I also don't want to hear that you just don't do relationships or you still want to be friends."

"Okay," Jaime said after a moment of silence. Sean could hear him take another deep breath. "Do you want me to get Lexi to drive the kids to rehearsals? She probably will."

"Yeah. If she's not going to show up and kill me." He'd never actually seen Aleksandra angry, but he'd heard stories.

"She won't. She likes you," Jaime said.

"Okay."

"Sean. I *am* sorry," Jaime said.

"I know." Sean wiped a hand over his face. His mom always said crying was healthy, but he'd never managed to use that logic to keep Travis from hovering. "I need you to hang up now. I don't actually want to."

"Okay. I'll let you know about Lexi and then I'll leave you alone, but I'm here if you change your mind about the friends thing, okay?"

"Yeah. Okay." Sean knew he was being dramatic holding the phone until Jaime hung up, but Steph had always said it was his dramatic nature that carried out from the stage.

It was a few minutes before his phone buzzed with a text.

Lexi agreed to drive next week. Also, she called me a stupid fucking asshole. In English. So she could be sure I understood.

Sean kind of hated that even if Jaime didn't want to be with him, he still knew how to make Sean smile. When Sean's phone buzzed again, it was from Alana.

Can we come in yet? Are you still on the phone? Travis won't let me listen at the door.

CHAPTER 7

TRAVIS LET him sleep until noon on Sunday with Alana curled up next to him before he walked in, grabbed the blankets, and took them into the living room. He did at least have the heart to dump them on the couch and not complain when that was as far as Sean and Alana moved.

"You're both going to class tomorrow and dress rehearsal. I'm considering making you both go to an extra class," Travis said as he stood in front of the TV at nine o'clock that night.

"You'd have to make Steph agree to it. She won't do that before a dress rehearsal," Sean said as Alana tried to see around Travis.

"If you don't move, I'm going to have to Google to find out if she stays married to the fourteen-year-old after she gets out of jail," Alana said before throwing a carrot stick at Travis.

"This is your one day. I swear, that's it. You're both getting up by eight tomorrow and your asses will be in class." Travis shook his head and left them, but he kept his word and woke them up early the next day. Of course, he also made breakfast and came to the studio with them when he didn't need to be there for two hours.

"YOU OKAY?" Alana slipped her hand into his as they peeked at the audience from behind the curtain at the first dress rehearsal two days later.

"I'm okay." Sean caught Aleksandra's eye for a second, and she gave him a small smile before he backed out of sight.

"Right. Let's do this, then."

If anything could take Sean's mind off Jaime, it was a stage. Extra rehearsals just made it easier. When he danced, everything he felt came out in his body and his movements. When he danced, it almost felt like the pain was worth something, but afterward the exhaustion just seemed heavier. By the last dress rehearsal on Thursday, he was grateful Alana and Travis each had a piece without him so he could get some time to himself.

"Who broke your heart?"

Sean started from his seat on the catwalk above the stage, where he was watching Travis direct a group of dancers from the safety of the shadows. Steph was getting older, but she still moved with a grace that let her sneak up on anyone.

"Travis told you?" He'd have been mad, but if Travis had adopted Alana, it was because Steph had adopted him first.

"No. Travis can block me out when he wants to, but you haven't made me tear up since you danced my Concerto Four with Travis and ended up on his couch a week later. I'd point out that mess of a relationship also made you so amazing at the audition that you got my attention, but I don't think you thought it was worth it at the time," Steph said as she sat next to him.

"Now that I know that's what got me in, it was worth it." Sean turned his head to look at her. "Is that what I'm supposed to learn right now? My heart gets broken, and my art is amazing, so it's worth it?"

"No." Steph shook her head and sighed. "I was just worried. I don't think there's actually an artist out there who has suffered real heartbreak and thought it was worth it. I don't think art comes from pain because pain is beautiful. Art that comes from pain is beautiful because it's what makes us capable of surviving it."

"This shouldn't even be that bad." Sean shook his head and leaned against the railing in front of him.

"Why? Feel whatever you want. Who cares if you should or shouldn't? People spend too much time telling each other how to feel."

"Thanks."

"Sleep tonight. Get rid of some of the dark circles." Steph stood and disappeared into the darkness.

CHAPTER 8

IT WAS early when Sean woke the next day to his phone vibrating next to him. Ten o'clock. The show wasn't until seven thirty. That meant he didn't have to be at the theater until five. Someone was dying for waking him up on a day Travis would let him sleep late.

It was Jaime. Five days of nothing, and now Jaime was waking him up when he should really know better. Sean stared at the glow of the new text alert without picking up the phone so he could read it.

It was probably nothing. It was probably a simple message to say good luck. It was possibly even a total mistake. Jaime had hit the wrong name, and he was going to get a sext meant for some other guy.

Sean slid his finger across the phone before his thoughts could get worse.

Can I come to the show tonight?

How was he supposed to answer that? After agreeing to disappear for a week, Jaime picked the day of the show to text him.

Why? Because Lupe wants you to?

Because I want to.

Sean stared at the screen. Maybe he could get Aleksandra's number and ask her to tell Jaime he was being confusing as hell. She seemed to like him enough.

I have no idea what you want me to think about that. I'm not awake enough to react well to this.

And now he wasn't going to be able to sleep anymore. Sean pushed back the blankets and climbed out of bed as his phone buzzed again. At least there would be the coffee Travis always made. The shower was running when he slipped into the living room, so he hurried to pour a cup of coffee and sneak back to his room before Travis could come out and ask why he was awake and complain that the coffee was just going to make him jittery and annoying. He took a sip before reading the next message.

Sorry. You don't have to answer. Or say yes.

The phone buzzed again in his hand as he finished reading.

I miss you.

Sean put the phone down and finished half the cup of coffee, and the message was still there when he picked the phone up again. When he couldn't come up with anything to type back for five minutes, he gave up and hit the call button.

"Hey," Jaime said, and then nothing.

"You never say hi when you answer the phone."

"I didn't know what else to say."

"Okay. How about you just tell me what's going on. How am I supposed to take this? That you miss your *friend*?"

"No."

Jaime paused, but Sean decided to wait him out instead of answering.

"No. I was stupid, and I'm sorry it took Lexi pointing it out five times a day for me to realize that. The guy at the club was just my friend. He was really just my friend, and I haven't been thinking about him at all for a week except that I was stupid to think you were the same when all I can do is miss you. I miss you telling me that I'm talented and I'm wasting it. I miss making a serving at dinner that isn't spicy, because you can't handle it. I miss waking up with you as much as I miss fucking you, and I'm going to hate it if I've lost you because it took me too long to figure that shit out. And I'm sorry for not realizing why you wanted me to come to the show tonight when you asked, but I get it now. And that's why I want to come."

Sean opened his mouth to answer, but couldn't come up with anything.

"Did I just make an idiot of myself?" Jaime asked.

"Do you care if you did?" Sean asked.

"Not really, but I'd feel better about it if it did me any good."

"It did." Sean took a deep breath. Alana and Travis were going to freak out. "I still want you to come, but we have to talk about this, and we won't have time tonight with the show and Lupe being there."

"Okay. I can come over tomorrow night if you want. After tomorrow's show, when there's no party. If you want me to."

"You'll come over here?" He hadn't realized it until the past week, but Jaime had never come to the city just to see him, even after avoiding Travis shouldn't have been an excuse anymore.

"Yeah. If Travis isn't going to kill me on sight now."

"Worry more about Alana. She's got nails."

Jaime was quiet for a moment before he asked, "You're joking, right?"

"I should probably warn them that I told you it was okay to come."

"I'm bringing Aleksandra."

Sean laughed for the first time since Alana had told him about Jaime's kiss in the club a week ago.

"I can control them when I need to," Sean said.

"Thanks. If you can't," Jaime said, "I know I kind of deserve it."

"I should probably argue with that, but I'm not awake enough to be a better person about it."

"That's okay. I'll see you tonight?" Jaime said.

"Yeah. We'll figure something out," Sean said before saying good-bye and hanging up.

Travis's knock on the door a minute later made him jump. He'd heard Travis walking around the living room while he was on the phone and he hadn't thought to lower his voice.

"You're up early," Travis said when he pushed the door open.

Sean held up his phone as an answer.

"Tell me it was your parents. They can get away with calling you too early," Travis said. When Sean shook his head, Travis brought his hand up to pinch the bridge of his nose. "Why did he call?"

"He wanted to apologize and ask if he could come to the show tonight."

"You didn't tell him no, did you?" Travis didn't need him to answer any more than he needed to hear what Travis had to say next. "Why do you do this to yourself?"

"I didn't just say yes. I said he could come tonight, but he needs to come over Saturday night when we have time to talk, and he said he will." Sean cut Travis off before he could speak. "If I want to give him another chance, I can give him another chance."

"What has he done to earn another chance?" Travis asked.

"What has he done that he doesn't deserve one? He didn't really cheat on me, and he didn't lie about anything." Sean looked up, even though he didn't want to see the disappointment on Travis's face.

"That's not an excuse, and I'm not clearing out Saturday, so you'll just have to stick to talking. I can't tell you what to do, but you know what I think about it." Travis turned and walked back into the living room as he called back, "You get to tell Alana yourself. And tell her I'm canceling the cable so I don't have to watch any more of your awful TV when this blows up."

"Good luck with that!" Sean called back. Alana loved him. Alana would not let Travis cancel their cable.

"IF YOU drop me on that third lift because you're trying to find him in the audience, I swear, I will injure you worse than Travis, and we'll just have to rework everything so he can dance it," Alana said when he told her about Jaime. He'd thought he was safe telling her right before the warm-up class, but no. Travis wasn't teaching it, so it was running late.

"No one does that. He'd have to be wearing a crazy bright light for me to even find him, and I've never dropped anyone on stage ever."

"But you've dropped me," Alana said as she pulled against him to stretch.

"One time."

"Two times," Alana corrected.

"I did not drop you twice. One time, you got dizzy, blacked out, and I put you down. If I'd dropped you, you would have had at least one bruise."

"Travis caught me."

"Travis helped me put you on the floor so I wouldn't drop you." Sean could have this argument without paying attention by now.

"So you would have dropped me if Travis hadn't caught me."

"You passed out during a lift because you didn't tell us you were sick. I might have been able to catch you myself, but that wasn't really a risk Travis felt like taking in the half second he had to think about it."

Alana shrugged as Steph came from backstage and waved for them all to line up.

"I'm coming over on Sunday morning for breakfast. If you're sad, I'm killing him."

"Travis says he's canceling the cable if that happens."

"I'll remind him about my DVD collection."

HEY. I'M here. Lexi and I have seats. Lupe has begun ushering. Good luck with everyone Michael seats. He's confused.

Sean smiled at the text as Alana groaned. The doors had only opened a few minutes ago, so he had to hope Michael would catch on as he typed a reply.

Thanks. I'll see you for a few minutes after the show?

"I'm taking your phone," Alana said as she typed into her own.

Lexi being here means we get to actually officially meet you guys after the show. Technically Travis met me once, but should I avoid this so Lupe doesn't figure something out?

Sean started to type back to ask when this had happened before he remembered Travis probably met Jaime at some point when they filled out paperwork for the internships.

If he does anything, Lupe won't have a clue.

When Sean looked up, Travis was standing by the winding staircase next to the stage, where he and Alana were sitting. He pointed at Sean's phone and held out his hand.

Travis is confiscating phones. I'll text after the show. Don't worry. I changed the passcode again.

It buzzed as he started to hand it to Travis, and Sean didn't need to look up to know Travis would be rolling his eyes as he pulled his phone back to read, *Break a leg,* before he locked the screen and let Travis snatch it out of his hand. Alana handed hers over without her usual fight—which was odd considering he was pretty sure they were supposed to have ten minutes left. She shrugged when he gave her a look.

"You were annoying me. Who did you think I was texting about it?"

SEAN WRAPPED Alana in his arms as soon as the curtains closed on the last bow, and they exchanged only one quick look before attacking Travis from either side. They were both still coated with sweat, and Travis was supposed to look respectable in his button-down shirt. He'd never been one to care, but he still pushed them off after a few seconds and directed them to get calmer hugs from Steph.

"You okay?" Sean asked him while Alana was out of earshot. "I know you miss it."

"Yeah. It's okay. Just a new dream. Making you show off my vision." Travis wrapped an arm around his neck and reached up to ruin his hair before shoving him away. "Go clean up or I'll be ready to check on the kids before you can get out there to protect your boy."

"Travis."

"I will behave with Lupe around. It is my job to be professional here. Tomorrow night, different story."

Sean considered arguing for only a second before turning toward the dressing rooms to wash off his makeup and change. He'd have to go without a shower because all he had to work with was a sink, but he'd picked up enough tricks to clean up from years of rushing to make himself presentable after performances. Twenty minutes later, he realized he still had to get his phone from Travis. All the other dancers probably had theirs, but then, they couldn't count on going home with Travis later and ending up with it.

When he stepped outside the dressing room feeling better in a clean silk shirt and dress pants, he found Alana already dressed in her cocktail dress outside the door on her phone.

"Too late. He went out to meet them a while ago. He sent them ahead to the party," Alana said without looking up from her phone.

"What?" The anger in his voice was enough to make Alana look up.

"Relax. He knew you'd insist on going with him. And then you'd see Jaime again for the first time with Lupe and Michael right there. You would have reacted. Even if Lupe wasn't paying attention, Michael might have seen it. Can you honestly tell me you could have pretended you'd never met him before? He's trying to protect you—both of you—for some reason I'm not even sure I get."

Sean started to argue, but she handed him back his phone. There was already a text waiting for him.

You were amazing. Lexi says you were beautiful.

Travis tried to break my hand via handshake, but I'm fine. Lexi has promised to distract Lupe for a few minutes at the party. Text me when you get there.

"You know we're right. Do you need me to take a picture of the face you make just from his texts to prove it to you?"

"No."

"We're not actually planning to keep you from seeing each other. Just maybe not for the first time again in front of people who don't know. Not when things have you so worked up that you're just projecting feelings all over the place."

"At the party. While Aleksandra is distracting Lupe and Michael." Sean looked up from the phone to see if she intended to keep that word.

"Sure. You're predictable. We knew you'd try it anyway," Alana said as her phone buzzed again. "Come on. I told Travis I'd take a cab with you since he read that story about the cab driver that was assaulting people. He doesn't want you to get attacked without me or whatever."

"If he's worried about cabs, he should worry more about you," Sean said as he pulled out his wallet to check for cash.

"I've never gotten assaulted or arrested for taking a dollar cab."

Sean toyed with his phone on the short cab ride to the hall they'd reserved.

"Just text him. If you're going be this worked up, we'll see if we can arrange it. I'd hate for you to not see him tonight at all and drop me tomorrow."

Sean didn't bother to argue as the cab pulled up to the curb to let them out. He just pulled the cash out of this wallet and handed it off.

"I should drive you places. You just tipped way too much." Alana shook her head as they stepped inside the doors but stopped short of entering the room.

I'm here. Can you get away?

Alana texted on her own phone while she waited for him. Probably to let Travis know they were there.

Yeah. Give me a minute and I'll meet you in the men's room. Lexi found a second one down the back hallway that no one is really using.

"Plan?" Alana asked.

"Why would I tell you?"

"Well, you could not tell me and try to sneak through a full party on your own because you are so great at that, or you can tell me where you're meeting him, and I can look upset and drag you there, and no one will interrupt us at all." Alana shrugged as if he really had a choice. It wasn't his fault people liked him and wanted to talk to him, so he tilted the phone so she could read the text message.

The plan was perfect, except the part were Alana hopped up on the counter inside the empty bathroom.

"What?" she asked when he glared at her. "I dragged you in here. If I leave, that's suspicious."

"You and Travis thought up this plan together," Sean said, though it was possible she had just picked that much up from being around Travis too much.

"Maybe," Alana admitted. "Because you wanted to see him tonight with Lupe and a lot of other people around, and you haven't had time to talk yet. Travis has already banned me from your apartment tomorrow night, but come on. If this blows up, or if Lupe catches you both in here with the whole company right outside? You're lucky Travis didn't get mad and point out why this was a really bad idea this morning."

Sean nodded. He still would rather have not had Alana sitting there when the door was pushed open and Jaime stepped through.

"Hey." Jaime's eyes locked on his, and he started to reach out to pull Sean closer before he stopped and moved to scratch the back of his neck instead. "Sorry. For everything. I don't know if you want me to...."

Jaime waved between them and sighed, and the insecurity in his eyes made it impossible for Sean not to take his hand to pull him closer.

"It's okay. Well, not all okay yet, but this is okay." Sean leaned closer, but instead of going straight for a kiss, he mirrored the move Jaime had used on him often and ducked to the side to let his face fall in the crook of Jaime's neck. Instead of leaving a tempting trail of kisses, he stayed there a few seconds breathing in the way Jaime's cologne mixed with his own personal scent. He let his hands rest on Jaime's hips as Jaime's arms came up around his back to hold him in.

"I'm so sorry. I'm so stupid," Jaime whispered as he moved one of his hands up to thread in Sean's hair.

"Well, okay. I can agree with that one." Alana's voice broke the moment, but Sean tightened his hold to keep Jaime from stepping back.

"Sorry. I didn't see you," Jaime said over his shoulder, but he gave up trying to pull away when Sean held on and groaned into Jaime's neck. He tried to remind himself that Alana was also the person who spent all of Sunday getting Travis to wait on them while they sat on the couch watching bad TV.

"Obviously—unless that display was to keep me from breaking your kneecaps or something."

"Alana." Sean gave in and pulled away from Jaime to glare at her.

"I didn't say I was actually going to break his kneecaps. Travis would kill me if I got arrested, and he couldn't post bail until tomorrow morning."

"Sorry. I don't think I can make her leave," Sean said as he turned his back on her. He'd had enough practice ignoring her, and Jaime had admitted to having a younger brother, so maybe he could just block her out also.

"It's okay. I kind of like having my kneecaps, so we don't have to try." Jaime gave him a small smile. He moved his hand toward Sean's, and when he hesitated, Sean reached out to catch his hand before Jaime could change his mind and shove his hands in his pockets. He threaded their fingers together and felt some of his own tension relax when Jaime didn't resist.

"Look." Sean took a deep breath and forced himself to keep talking although he knew he might be ending everything. "I'm not really mad, and I understand dating around, but I don't really want to do that anymore. Well, I wasn't, but I get why you were."

"Sean." Jaime's voice was soft, but Sean shook his head before Jaime could continue. If he didn't finish this now, he wouldn't be able to say it later, and then Alana would either butt in or tell Travis. Probably both.

"Just let me finish," Sean said, and Jaime nodded and squeezed the hand he was holding. "I'm just past the point of being okay with that. So I need to know that's not what's going on anymore. You don't have to just say yes because you came tonight if you're not sure, but that's what I need if you're coming back tomorrow."

"Look at me?" Jaime asked, tugging a little at the hand Sean had been staring at while he talked. "I haven't done this in a long time. I haven't met anyone that made me want to, and I'm sorry I didn't figure out that I wanted this until I almost lost it, but I'm there. There's no one else I'm attached to."

"You're sure?" Sean asked as Jaime moved his free hand to the back of his neck. His thumb brushed over Sean's cheek.

"I'm sure." Jaime's hand on his neck urged him closer, but it was gentle enough to give Sean the choice to close the distance. Sean didn't hesitate any longer before moving to bring their lips together. Jaime lost his hesitation and deepened the kiss, nipping at Sean's bottom lip because he knew it always made Sean give in completely.

"Still here. Still in a public place," Alana called behind them.

Jaime broke the kiss, but he didn't step away as he pressed his face against Sean's neck to compose himself.

"*Te veías tan guapo.*" Jaime breathed the words into his throat before pulling back. Sean didn't bother asking him to translate. If he never did for Sean, he wouldn't in front of Alana.

"Travis says he's already introduced all the donors to every other principal and soloist, and he can only push the interns at them so much when they're the ones paying us. He would like us to remember that we're expected to smile and pretend to be interested in something they have to say besides the money they give to the arts so that they'll write him some more checks." Alana typed something into her phone and hopped off the counter. "We really have to get out there."

"Sorry." Sean kept himself from asking Jaime to come up with a reason to stay while Aleksandra drove Lupe and Michael home.

"It's okay. I'll see you tomorrow. I'll probably take them soon since we have to drive back."

Sean leaned in for one more kiss before Alana took his arm and dragged him away and out of the bathroom.

CHAPTER 9

SEAN LET the hot water sluice through his hair and over the sore muscles of his shoulders. He was lingering in the shower longer than he should. Sean had come back to the apartment with Travis and had plenty of time to be out of the shower before Jaime was expected to show up, but he hadn't rushed the way he should have.

He heard a knock on the door, but he stayed under the spray and let Travis get the door. A week ago, he would have rushed to the door to pull Jaime past Travis, but even with the hope that Jaime meant everything he'd said, Sean didn't trust himself not to take one look at Jaime and forgive everything the way he'd wanted to the night before. He needed the extra minutes to strengthen his own resolve, anyway. He heard Travis say something as he dried off and smoothed moisturizer over his face, but he couldn't make out the words.

Travis was on the other side of the bathroom door when Sean opened it. He blocked Sean's view before Sean could look past him to find Jaime, and let his hand rest on Sean's shoulder as he leaned close enough that Sean could hear him at the lower volume.

"I'll stay in my room, but just let me know if you want me to kick him out or you need anything."

"I know." Sean brought his hand up to rest on Travis's wrist for a second before pushing him away.

Travis nodded, but he turned back to where Sean could now see Jaime standing by the couch.

"He has to be up at eight-thirty for the matinee tomorrow. It's already ten. Don't keep him up all night."

Sean pushed Travis away and toward his room.

"You're not my babysitter or my mother."

Travis just laughed as he left and called back, "Your mom loves me. She'd be on my side."

Sean shook his head as he turned to Jaime.

"Sorry. You can ignore that." Sean nodded toward his room when Jaime didn't answer. "I should probably put on more than a towel."

"If the plan is to talk, that's probably a good idea." Jaime finally gave him the smirk Sean was used to, but it didn't carry to his eyes.

Jaime followed Sean to his room, but paused at the door instead of following Sean inside.

"Are you really going to lose the ability to talk if you watch me change?" Sean asked.

"I wasn't sure you wanted me to." Jaime came in and closed the door behind him.

"Oh. I've been changing in front of rooms of people for so long I don't really think about it. I don't even notice when I change in front of Alana." Sean pulled a pair of loose gray sweatpants from the top shelf his closet. He glanced over his shoulder as he took off the towel and hung it up. As Sean pulled on the sweatpants, Jaime had averted his eyes to study the bracelets and leather cuffs Sean had left on his dresser. "Should I be worried you're not watching? I do actually notice when *you* watch me."

"No," Jaime said as he looked up from his examination of the medallion on the leather wrap bracelet that had been Sean's favorite the last few months. "I just wasn't fully joking about not being able to think."

Jaime moved toward him slowly enough to give Sean time to back away. When he didn't, Jaime stepped into his space and let his eyes drift down to the defined muscles of Sean's abdomen. His eyes flicked to Sean's before moving back down as he lifted his right hand to place it flat against Sean's bare stomach. He left it there for a few seconds, just stroking feather light with his thumb as Sean sucked in a breath, and then grazed his hand up the side of Sean's chest. Jaime's eyes followed his hand as his thumb rubbed around and over Sean's nipple. He only looked up to meet Sean's eyes when Sean let a harsh gasp escape his lips.

"Right." Sean knew his voice was rough as he pulled back and turned away. "I'll just find a shirt, and you can take off your shoes, because I don't have a foot fetish, and your dirty boots aren't getting on my bed."

Jaime chuckled behind him as Sean took more time to find a T-shirt than he really needed. This was why he'd let Travis talk to Jaime. Left alone, Sean just wanted to give in and let Jaime take him apart with his touch. When he turned around, Jaime was reclining on his bed with his back propped up on the black leather headboard, but it was far from his normal relaxed sprawl.

Sean crawled onto the bed to lie next to him on his side, but left a safe amount of space between them.

"I really didn't think you were going to come back after last week. I wasn't even sure after last night that you'd really show up tonight," Sean said as picked at a thread on his comforter.

"I know. I didn't plan to—after last week. After last night, there was nothing that would have kept me from being here tonight." Jaime met his eyes when Sean looked up and reached out to take his hand.

"Why did you? You didn't seem like you were going to change your mind last week. You seemed pretty sure about what you wanted."

"I thought I was." Jaime paused and ran his free hand over his buzz cut. "Sean, I haven't had a real relationship in a few years. It's not because I'm against it or anything. I'm just not going to start something serious just to do it. I don't *need* to be with someone. But I want to be with you. I just didn't figure it out as fast as you wanted me to. I know that sucked. I know I shouldn't have had to lose you and be miserable and have Lexi leave pictures she took of you at rehearsal all over the apartment to figure it out."

"She did that?"

"It's really unfair. She hates everyone. When did you brainwash her onto your side?"

"I didn't know I had." As far as he remembered, Aleksandra had barely even talked to him.

"You just have no idea how you get under people's skin, do you?" Jaime slid down the bed so he was lying on his side facing Sean. "I couldn't even get mad at her for calling me an ass because I agreed with her. I kept asking her how you were doing after every rehearsal until she pointed out that I should ask myself why I cared so much, or why I got so pissed when she told me you were talking to some other guy."

"She told you I was talking to another guy?" Sean tried to think of another dancer Aleksandra might have seen him talking to, but she'd really only had the chance to see him talk to Travis and Michael. Jaime studied him for a second before groaning.

"She made that up, didn't she?" Jaime looked at him with a mix of annoyance and hope.

"I can't even think of where she would have gotten the idea."

"There was really never another guy?" Jaime asked, like he actually had a reason to need more of a confirmation.

"There was never another guy for *me*." Sean felt bad for his emphasis when Jaime's relieved face fell. "Sorry. I know you didn't really do anything wrong."

"No." Jaime shook his head and looked down at their linked hands. "I did. Lexi told me I should have known better. Even before she knew you'd found out. She saw me kiss Juan at the club, and she asked me that night what was wrong with me. When I told her we weren't serious, she asked if I was sure you knew that. And Alana wouldn't have told on me if she didn't know you'd be upset. I should have known how you felt because everyone else did, and I deserved how I felt when Lexi told me some other guy was already going after you and I had lost my chance."

"You didn't lose your chance, but I have to know it's just me, and you're not going to get drunk and kiss someone else." Sean knew he had tightened his grip on Jaime's hand like he could hold him there, but he couldn't make himself let go as he said it.

"Sean, I know, but it wasn't because I was drunk. I didn't realize it would hurt you, but it didn't mean anything. It was just a stupid drunk kiss on the dance floor with a friend that I didn't think enough about. You mean something. I get that now. I'm not going to fuck that up." Jaime squeezed his hand. "I can't promise I'm going to get everything perfect, but I won't cheat. You have to know this wasn't a sign I'm going to cheat."

"Okay." Sean nodded. Travis would probably say he was forgiving too quickly, but if he didn't trust Jaime, it wouldn't work. Still, he couldn't help asking. "So you're still friends with that guy?"

"Yeah." Jaime slipped his hand out of Sean's grip to hold the side of his face.

"He's just a friend. We've never even dated. I'm kind of hoping you can get that, because we've been friends a long time. When Lexi told him about you, he was really pissed he was even involved in hurting you. I'm pretty sure he will never kiss me in a club again, even if you dump me right now. I had to beg Lexi not to tell him your last name or what company you were with, because he threatened to show up at one of your shows to explain it wasn't his fault."

"He probably wouldn't have gotten past Travis anyway." Sean felt his own smile as he gave in to the urge to move closer so they were pressed against each other with his face against Jaime's neck, where he could breathe in the scent he'd been missing.

Jaime wrapped his arms around him and threaded his fingers through Sean's hair.

"*Te eché mucho de menos y no voy a dejar que te vayas.*" Jaime breathed more than spoke the words into his ear.

"Will you translate this time?" Sean wasn't sure why he whispered back, only to feel Jaime shake his head. "Why do you do that? Say things to me I can't understand and not translate—besides because it turns me on. I don't think that's what you were going for this time."

"Does it bother you? I can stop doing it."

"If it bothered me, it probably wouldn't get the reaction you're going for when we're having sex. I don't think you're actually insulting me. I'm just curious." Sean pressed his lips to Jaime's neck before looking up at him with the expression that could even get Travis to give him what he wanted most of the time. It had worked on Jaime before, but this time he looked away like that was the only way to avoid giving in, so Sean looked back down.

"Sometimes it's just easier to say what I want to say to you if you can't understand me."

"That doesn't make sense, but I'm used to people with logic that doesn't make sense, so I understand." Sean let himself relax with the light laugh he felt where he was pressed against Jaime's chest. "Whenever you're ready to translate, you can just tell me."

"It's late. I think I'm supposed to be letting you sleep." Jaime's fingers leaving soft trails over his back made him want to agree, but it still wasn't what he was expecting. Out of all the nights he'd spent at Jaime's apartment, they'd never gone to sleep without having sex.

"Did Travis actually scare you out of trying to have sex tonight? I'm never leaving him alone with you again if that's going to keep happening."

"No. You just seem worn out, but if you want to, I'm not turning you down," Jaime said, but he pressed a kiss to the top of Sean's head and didn't change the calming strokes on Sean's back. "So you're admitting you took a long shower and left me to get attacked by Travis on purpose?"

"Are you mad?"

"No. I deserved it. You had every right to be mad. I just wanted to know for sure if you did it on purpose." Jaime hugged him tighter for a second.

"I didn't do it because I was mad," Sean said. Part of him regretted inviting more questions when Jaime stilled before pulling away to try and study his face.

"Then why?" Jaime asked.

Sean ducked his head back down to Jaime's chest before he answered.

"I really wanted you back, and I'm not always great at saying what I need to say. If you'd come in and just tried to skip talking and get me in bed, I probably would have let you without making you promise anything. I knew Travis would say everything important if I couldn't." When Jaime didn't answer right away, Sean added, "Sorry if that came with threats about how he can hide your body."

"It was more of a threat about letting Alana claw my eyes out if I made you cry again, but that's okay. I deserved that one."

"He told you I cried? I'm going to kill him."

"Babe, I heard you on the phone. If it happened more than that, I really deserved the threat." Jaime pulled back so he could run the back of his hand down Sean's cheek and tilt Sean's head up so Sean had to look at him. "Don't let me hurt you because you don't want to tell me I'm doing it. I'll let Travis corner me on purpose if I think you're doing that."

"You're a masochist."

"I'm not pretending that's preferred. I'd really like it better if you told me yourself." He leaned down to press their lips together and Sean couldn't help pressing closer, but Jaime kept the kiss soft and pulled back as Sean tried to follow his lips. "Let me get the lights and get in bed. Then if you don't want to sleep, I'm not going to fight you."

Sean heard Jaime shucking off his jeans after he'd flicked off the light, and when he joined Sean under the blankets, he'd taken off his shirt as well. Sean couldn't resist running his hands over the light hair on Jaime's chest, but he couldn't pretend his eyes weren't drooping as he settled into his favorite spot in Jaime's arms with his head pillowed on Jaime's shoulder. He felt the light pressure of a kiss on the top of his head as he started to drift off.

SEAN WOKE up to the calming sensation of Jaime's fingers running through his hair and down his back. He resisted waking up and curled closer, pressing his face into Jaime's neck to block out the light.

"Come on. Wake up." Jaime's voice was soft, but not enough for Sean to ignore him and drift back to sleep. "It's almost eight thirty, and I don't think you remembered to set an alarm."

Sean turned away from him in an attempt to get more sleep, but he still pulled on Jaime's arm to make him turn on his side so he was spooned behind Sean like a warm, heavy blanket. He felt the hot puff of a laugh on the back of his neck.

"Babe, I can't bribe you with breakfast. I'm not even sure you have food and pans I could work with. If you do, you have to get up with me and show them to me." Jaime pulled him onto his back and pressed kisses up his neck before nipping at his earlobe. "Next time you ask me why I got up without you, I'm going to point out how much work this is. Now that I've tried waking you up, I have an excuse to let you sleep late."

Sean decided a shrug was enough of a response. He'd only half complained once, and that was before he'd realized that if Jaime got up without him, breakfast would already be finished when he stumbled out of the bedroom.

"I'm about to take this as a sign that I should start trying to wake you up earlier than ten minutes before you're supposed to be up."

Sean was pretty sure he could hear the teasing in Jaime's voice, but he cracked his eyes open anyway.

"Hey," Jaime whispered when their eyes met.

Sean was still trying to wake up to answer when Travis knocked hard enough to shake the door.

"It's eight thirty! You've got five minutes to show some signs of life, because Alana is on her way over. I'm not pulling you out of bed myself if you're naked," Travis called through the door.

"I'm already awake!" Sean yelled back as he groaned and shuffled closer to Jaime under the covers.

"You don't even own an alarm, do you?" Jaime asked after a few seconds.

"I've had to use my phone a couple times when he was out of town." Sean turned on his side and backed away enough that his morning breath wouldn't be in Jaime's face.

"I'm not sure if that makes him overbearing or you completely spoiled," Jaime said.

"Depends on who you ask."

"Right. So in the future, I should just yell at you?"

"I'd rather you stick with your method, or just let me sleep and move to breakfast in bed." Sean would really rather sleep until two, but if he had to get up, Jaime kissing up his neck as he woke up made it suck a lot less.

"You're losing your argument against being completely spoiled." Jaime smiled and shook his head as he started to pull back the blankets.

"It's way too early in this relationship for you to start siding with Travis."

Jaime froze in his movements just long enough for Sean to notice something was off. He started to push back the blankets the rest of the way, but Sean caught his wrist before he could climb out of bed.

"Hey," Sean said to make Jaime look back at him. Jaime only met his eyes for a second before looking away, but it was enough for Sean to see some panic. "Are you freaking out on me?"

"Maybe a little." Jaime took a deep breath, but he caught Sean's hand when he started to pull back. "Just a little. Not a lot. It's okay. It just hasn't all sunk in yet."

"Are you sure? I know I kind of rushed you." Sean wasn't sure what he'd do if Jaime said he needed more time.

"I'm sure." Jaime looked at him. His eyes still held some fear, but it didn't seem to be coupled with doubt. "I don't want anyone else. I just need to get used to all the labels and extra stuff, but it's fine."

"Okay. That stuff isn't important. We can give that time," Sean said, although part of him just wanted to hear Jaime introduce him to anyone as his boyfriend. "Just try to call me if you go home and freak out completely."

"Lexi will probably call you for me." Jaime squeezed his hand just as Travis yelled through the door again that Alana would be there with bagels any minute.

"You seriously don't have a lock on your door?" Jaime reached for his jeans to pull them on.

"Alana figured out how to pick it a long time ago." Sean gave him time to throw on his shirt and went out to the living room just as Travis opened the door for Alana.

"You want the bathroom?" Sean asked Jaime as Travis took the bags of food to the breakfast bar.

"You should say yes, or you'll never get a chance," Alana interrupted before Jaime could answer. "He'll try to rush through his hair and his eight million products, and he'll be at least twenty minutes."

Jaime looked at him like he wasn't sure if he should argue that Sean hadn't done that at his apartment, but maybe he knew Sean had enough sense not to take over his bathroom before he'd officially heard the word *boyfriend*.

"I can manage fifteen." It was possible if he rushed, and his hair liked him this morning.

"Right." Jaime turned toward the bathroom and closed the door behind him.

"Can you please just not freak him out this morning?" Sean kept his voice down. "We talked. He's not seeing anyone else, and he's not going to, so can you both just pretend you're nice people?"

"You think he's going to freak out in twenty minutes?" Only Travis could look judgmental with a bagel half in his mouth.

"No, but it's early, and he needs coffee. And I already let you give him the third degree for over fifteen minutes last night, and he stayed, so you can give him a break," Sean said to Travis as he got a mug and poured some coffee before turning to Alana. "And Travis threatened to let you claw his eyes out, and you already threatened to break his kneecaps Friday night. You can be nice for fifteen minutes."

Jaime looked nervous as he stepped out of the bathroom, but he smiled when Sean met him with the mug of coffee.

"Technically, you could stand in the bathroom to drink this while I do my hair if you want."

"Thanks." Jaime smiled around the cup as he took a drink. "But I can handle it."

"I'll try to hurry."

Sean was pretty sure he'd set a record, but he still found an awkward silence at the breakfast bar when he came out. At least Jaime had a bagel, so they'd decided not to make him starve.

"I don't know how to not freak him out. I just told him about that movie we were watching on Lifetime the other day. I thought movies were safe," Alana said.

"I'm fine. I'm not freaked out," Jaime said, but he didn't sound so sure.

"Also, I stole twenty bucks out of your wallet to pay for breakfast."

CHAPTER 10

SEAN WOULD have liked to have more time with Jaime the next week. Instead he had a full week of classes and Jaime had two projects due, so he had to make do with texts, short calls, and Travis rolling his eyes when Jaime tried to spy on his Tuesday class.

When his phone rang with a number he didn't recognize Wednesday night, he answered only because Alana was using Travis as her own personal cook, and if he didn't answer, she'd take his phone to see who it was.

"Your boyfriend is an idiot," Aleksandra said after he answered. She skipped pleasantries faster than Jaime, but her slight Russian accent was unmistakable. "I need you to fix him tomorrow before I move back to Russia to get away from him."

"What's wrong?" Sean hadn't heard from Jaime all day, but between his morning classes at the studio and Jaime's night class at school, it hadn't worried him.

"He's—" Aleksandra paused as she tried to think of the right words for what she wanted to say. Her English was almost perfect, but sometimes she seemed to get stuck on stringing the right words together for descriptions. "He's thinking too much. All the time."

"Thinking about what?"

"Everything." Aleksandra sighed. "I can't even keep track. One minute he's trying to figure out exactly how to make you happy, the next he starts going on about how he can't be everything you want him to be. I'd blame you for making crazy demands, but as he doesn't seem to know what they are, I believe he's making these things up. If he is not fixed after you see him tomorrow, I'm driving him right back to the city and leaving him at your door."

As threats went, Sean had heard five from Alana in the past few hours that were a lot worse than forcing him to spend the night with Jaime, but that didn't mean he shouldn't try to figure out the issue anyway. Sean ignored the looks Travis and Alana gave him as he stood from his seat at the bar and moved to his room.

"Can you give me some examples?"

"You need examples?" Aleksandra might like him enough to call him, but her tone didn't convey much faith.

"He really hasn't said anything to me to make me think anything is wrong. If you can give me some idea of what he's saying to you, it will be easier for me to try and fix things." Sean refrained from pointing out that she had to suspect this, or she wouldn't be calling him.

Aleksandra was quiet for a moment, and Sean almost gave up and started guessing when she spoke.

"I think maybe he doesn't remember how to be with someone, so he thinks it's a lot more complicated than it is, and he won't tell you the million things he's unsure about because he already messed up once, and he thinks he has to be perfect now."

"I never said he had to be perfect." It came out softer than he planned, but Aleksandra must have heard him anyway.

"I didn't really think you did, but maybe you could make sure he knows that. Because right now, he's so scared he's going to do something wrong that he's not even enjoying having you. I had to scream at him that you were not going to be mad if he didn't call you tonight because he has a three-hour class tonight and an early day tomorrow. Yesterday he started saying that calling you his boyfriend was too much of a commitment, and then three hours later he was worried that you hate children, and he's always assumed he'd have kids." Aleksandra paused, and then continued when he didn't say anything. "And I really should not have told you those last two. Pretend I didn't say that."

"It's okay." Sean sat on his bed as he tried to process everything. "It's probably better that you said both of them and not just one or the other. Balances things out."

"Are you worrying about stupid things now too? I have Alana's number."

"No." Sean probably said it too quickly, but Alana was already in the apartment, and she'd repeat everything to Travis. "I'm just not sure how to fix all that in a date that's only a couple hours tomorrow."

"You probably can't, but if you can convince him that it's okay to call you and talk to you about it when he starts worrying about stupid things, I can probably not go back to Russia. Also tell him you aren't going to dump him if he's not perfect. Right now, I can't even get him to call you and ask you about stupid stuff like if you want him to sleep at your place again Saturday night because you have a show Sunday afternoon, or if you want to come here like you usually do. He's also worried that you won't want to do either because you're busy, and he doesn't want to admit he misses you."

"Well, at least one of those is easy to fix tomorrow," Sean said. If Travis argued that he needed his sleep, he was going to point out that he'd sleep better if Jaime wore him out.

"Great. If he is less annoying tomorrow night, I will even volunteer to drive the kids back and forth so you have more time. If he's more annoying, I'm handcuffing him to your bed until you figure something out."

WHEN SEAN turned the corner the next day to walk toward Jaime's car, the November weather was cold enough that Jaime's leather jacket was zipped, but he still stood outside the car instead of waiting inside where it was warmer. Soon it would be too cold for them to meet outside, where the street was empty enough to feel like they had a few minutes alone. Sean was only a few steps away when Jaime heard him and looked away from his phone. He smiled, but Sean could see tension there that hadn't been present a few weeks ago. Still, Jaime pulled him in once he was within reach, and Sean felt some of his own nerves drain out as they kissed. Jaime let him pull back sooner than he had in the past, but that just made Sean move back in for more. The third time, Jaime laughed against his lips.

"Are you actually going to take me up on the backseat this time?" Jaime tightened his grip on Sean's waist to pull their hips together, and Sean almost gave in. Somehow it had been almost three weeks since they'd had sex, and that hadn't seemed so long until Jaime was in front of him again.

"No. I can admit I almost considered it this time, but still no." Sean pulled away and held out his hand. "Coffee?"

Jaime only hesitated a second before threading their fingers together, but it was long enough for Sean to see it. When he didn't let go on the walk to a coffee shop, all Sean could hear was Aleksandra's voice in his head telling him Jaime thought he had to be perfect—which would mean holding Sean's hand whether he wanted to or not.

Sean let his hand go as they went through the door without glancing back to see if Jaime reacted to it.

"I can get it," Jaime said, putting his hand out to stop him when Sean reached for his wallet after ordering.

"You don't have to." He would appreciate the gesture more if he wasn't doubting everything Jaime did.

"I want to." Jaime gave him a look that was half-lost, like Sean was rejecting him though he would have been happy about the offer two weeks ago. The barista looked back and forth between them as she tried to decide whose card to take.

"Yeah. Sure." Sean agreed, because they needed to talk, but a four-dollar cup of tea was not worth trying to do it while holding up a line of people.

Sean led them to a table in the back corner. It was far from private, but better than the counter by the windows. He fiddled with the cardboard sleeve on his cup as he tried figure out how bring up any of the things Aleksandra had thrown at him. He'd just about decided to start by making it clear how much he wanted Jaime to come over on Saturday when Jaime spoke up.

"Was that bad? Am I not supposed to buy your drink?"

"No. It's fine if you want to." When Sean looked up from his cup, Jaime met his eyes.

"I said I wanted to."

"Okay." Sean took a deep breath. Even if Aleksandra hadn't called him, he would have read the insecurity in Jaime's eyes. He just would have been lost on what it was about. "So if you want to come over Saturday, I want you to. I don't have time to come to you because we close the show in New York on Sunday, but if you can stay, I want you to. It feels like I haven't gotten to sleep with you in forever."

"I can work that out somehow. It might be late if I have to drive Lupe home first." Jaime smiled with just a hint of the cocky smile Sean knew was going to lead to another invitation into the car.

"Aleksandra said she'd do it." Sean blurted it out before he could talk himself out of it. It was probably not how she wanted him to start the conversation, but it seemed worse to make Jaime think he was psychic while Jaime couldn't figure anything out on his own. Jaime stared at him a second before he pulled away. Sean hadn't even noticed he was leaning over the table toward him until Jaime was leaning away from him and pressing back against the wall instead.

"She called you." Jaime crossed his arms over his chest.

"I was probably not supposed to tell you, but it felt like lying not to," Sean admitted, but it didn't seem to make Jaime less closed off, so he tried again. "Yes, she mentioned you might want an invite for Saturday, but I was going to do it anyway. It just saved me the time I was going to spend planning out how to talk you into making the trip again so soon."

"But there was a plan?" Jaime seemed to relax just a little at the suggestion.

"Yes. It probably would have ended with me making out with you until you couldn't think and promising you sex on Saturday." Sean shrugged. "Sorry. I think I would have chickened out on just asking you and gone with the classic."

"Tease." Jaime smirked as he leaned forward again.

"It seems to work for me."

"But asking worked too." Jaime's smile dropped a bit as he added, "Did she say anything else?"

"She might have said a few other things." Sean caught his wrist before he could close off again. "Can I say at least a few things before you shut me out?"

"I'm not. I know it's not your fault she called you," Jaime said. He didn't look back at Sean, but he didn't try to pull his wrist free from Sean's grasp either. "But I don't even know what she said, and if I wanted to talk to you about something, she should have let me do it myself. I'm sure Alana wanted to kill me last week, but she and Travis let you deal with it mostly. And I'm sure Travis knew he had your permission when he talked to me. She doesn't know when to mind her own business."

"Would you have talked to me if she hadn't?"

"Eventually." Jaime flipped his hand over so he could hold Sean's hand across the table. At least Sean didn't doubt that he wanted to do it this time. "Can you just tell me what she said so I know what this conversation is about? She was probably overdramatic."

"Okay." Sean took a few seconds to sort out the main points in his head. If he chose to forget the part about the children, he was sure Jaime would appreciate that. "She said you've been worrying about various things and not telling me because you think you already messed up too much. She thinks you think you have to be perfect now, and that's keeping you from talking to me."

When Jaime didn't argue, Sean figured that was enough confirmation.

"You don't have to be perfect. What happened with Juan is over. Yes, I want to meet him at some point, but I trust you, and I don't want you pushing yourself to do things because you think you have to. It's okay if you want to buy my drink as long as you really want to do it— and as long as you let me buy you coffee or dinner sometimes too. If you're uncomfortable holding my hand when we're walking, you can say that instead of just doing it to make me happy."

"I'm not. I'm just not used to it," Jaime interrupted, and followed his statement by squeezing Sean's hand. "I can get used to some things that make you happy if they don't really bother me."

"But if they do, you can tell me. Or if you just need things to be slower or you're not sure what I'm thinking, you can just ask me. I'm not just going to get frustrated or anything like that. Okay?" Sean rubbed his thumb in circles on Jaime's wrist until he nodded.

"Okay. I'll try to remember that maybe I needed to hear that when I go home and yell at her." Jaime released his hand to pick up his coffee and take a drink. "On that note, can we talk about something else now? I'll tell you if something's bothering me, but we kind of just covered a lot when I wasn't prepared. So can we just relax and talk about something else? I'm sure there is some story about Alana you can tell me."

"She's been too nice this week. Last time she was this nice for this long, we realized a week later she'd taken a sky diving class and was trying not to tell us about it." Sean laughed as Jaime's eyes widened.

"Why did she ever tell you?"

"She cut her arm landing. She was fine, but Travis started freaking out that someone attacked her until she caved. So I don't have any new stories this week, but I'll probably have something soon."

"I'm going to have nightmares about Lupe hanging out with her."

CHAPTER 11

"ALANA SAYS I was supposed to get whole cloves instead of ground. Does that ruin everything?" Sean asked as he let Jaime in the apartment. He should have known mentioning Jaime could cook would make Alana crash their plans Saturday night. All he wanted to do was pull Jaime into the bedroom and make up for all the time they'd lost in the last two weeks, but Alana had started in on how his friends barely knew his boyfriend, and it wasn't worth the fight.

"I can work with it. Don't worry." Jaime leaned in for a kiss, but it was over earlier than Sean would have liked as Jaime looked over his shoulder to where Alana and Travis were watching from the bar.

"I can't believe you even let Sean buy ingredients. He should have taken me with him, or Travis at least," Alana said. Travis just gave Jaime a nod before moving to the couch to watch TV instead.

"I can make something work if there's stuff missing." Jaime looked through the groceries Sean had left out on the counter.

"He didn't know the fish had to thaw until I told him." Alana smiled back when Sean glared at her. "He probably didn't know that snapper was fish. I'm sure he just asked at the store."

Jaime was biting his lip to keep from laughing, but he handed Alana a cutting board and the garlic to chop. Sean thought about objecting to giving her a knife, but it did give her something to do instead of talk as Jaime squeezed the juice out of the limes and lemons. Sean decided not to point out it would have been less work to just buy juice in a bottle. It couldn't make that much of a difference if he was just going to mix everything together and throw it in the refrigerator.

"When you asked what kind of pans he had, I had to explain that it mattered. He also thought pots and pans were two words for the same thing, so telling him you needed a sauté pan was kind of a waste of time." Alana was evil. She could make him sound like a moron and cut an onion without crying at the same time. For someone who always made Travis cook for her, she was chopping vegetables as fast as Jaime gave them to her.

Sean could tell Jaime tried for a few seconds before he gave up his attempts not to laugh. To his credit, he regained control after only a few seconds of Sean glaring at both of them.

"Babe, I'm sorry. My mama kind of taught me that when I was three or four," Jaime said. "I promise in a week Lexi will have forgiven you for telling on her, and she'll think up something worse about me."

"I just don't cook."

"We don't let him." Alana stopped when he kicked her. "And I won't explain why right now, so you'll just have to trust me. He was learning other things when he was four. Like every single type of dance there is and how to play the violin and how to swim."

"You did all that when you were four?" Jaime glanced back at Alana like he was trying to figure out if she was making stuff up before turning around to work at the stovetop.

"It was piano, not violin, but yeah. My mom liked putting me in classes. She figured she'd give me a lot of options and see what I liked."

"And she didn't put you in a Spanish class?" Jaime asked. "I'm not judging. I'm just wondering if you're lying about not understanding anything."

"I wasn't really good at languages," Sean said after a second.

"You were four. How were you good at anything?" Jaime asked, shaking his head as he took the board of vegetables from Alana to add to the sauce he'd already mixed.

"I was extra bad at languages." Sean shrugged. The clicking of the spoon against the bowl paused for just long enough that he knew Jaime had caught the shift in his voice. It seemed more dramatic if Sean made him ask, so he added, "I had a lisp. So I was in speech therapy for a long time. I had a hard enough time speaking English, so I took Latin in high school to get my language credit out of the way. They don't make you speak that in front of people. It's just reading and writing."

"I was in ESL until fifth grade," Jaime said after a few seconds. He turned to the stove, and Sean couldn't see his face as he transferred the fish from the mixture in the bowl. Alana kept her mouth shut for once, so they only heard sizzling for a few minutes until Jaime added, "I knew some English when I started school, but only what my mom knew and what my older brother had taught me. It wasn't a lot."

"Your English is perfect. You don't even have an accent. Well, unless you're speaking Spanish."

"Yours is just as perfect." Jaime was smiling when he looked back at him. "You're sure it doesn't bother you when I speak Spanish?"

"No. You're probably going to get away with it as long as you want, because I'm not going to pick it up. I barely passed Latin in high school, and I think my teacher just felt bad for me. I'm never going to get past *hello* and *good-bye*."

"I know some Spanish. What's he saying? Wait. Do I want to know? Is he saying dirty things in Spanish in bed?" Alana paused and tilted her head. "Yes. I definitely want to know."

"I don't really remember. I think he called me crazy once." Even if Sean could remember the words, he wasn't about to mess up the pronunciation with Jaime listening. Also, if Jaime was saying things he wasn't ready to fully share with Sean, then Sean wasn't going to repeat them to Alana. "I assume everything else is just about how amazing I am."

"It's probably about how annoying you are," Alana said as she pulled out her phone. "He doesn't want to hurt your feelings, so he says it in Spanish to get the frustration out. I will Google the Spanish words for 'annoying,' 'spends too much time on his hair,' and 'lazy.' Maybe he said, 'You are crazy and annoying because you use too many hair products.'"

"I didn't call you crazy." Jaime smirked as he set plates in front of them. "I promise."

"You should have." Alana speared a piece of fish with her fork and moaned. "This is amazing. You need to come over every week."

"Thanks." Jaime ducked his head with a shy smile at the compliment, as he turned away to make another plate. He nodded to where Travis was still watching TV on the couch. Alana rolled her eyes and picked up her own plate with the new one to carry to the couch. She pushed the plate into his hands and said something too low for them to pick up.

"Should I be worried he still hates me?" Jaime whispered.

"He doesn't." Sean sighed when Jaime mouthed, *Really.* "I don't think it's all you this time. He's been off the last few days. I think the girl he had a couple dates with kind of dropped off."

Sean shook his head at Jaime's questioning look. Travis would say something about it eventually, and whispering about him from across the apartment wouldn't help.

"How often do you make breakfast for Aleksandra?" Sean asked after a few more bites of his dinner.

"Every day but Tuesday and Thursday? She has a really early class those days. I make extra if I'm cooking anyway, but I'm not getting up to cook for her. Why?" Jaime looked up from his plate just before Sean ducked his head down. Jaime reached out to rest his hand on Sean's wrist. "You're the one who told me not to shut you out."

"He thought you made breakfast for him," Travis said as walked past. His plate clattered in the sink over the silence that had set in.

"You're not helping, and now you're just being mean," Alana said.

"Yeah." Travis sighed and pinched the bridge of his nose. "Sorry. It's been a long week. But the food was good. I can do dishes if you guys want to leave them."

"It's fine. Just let me get there by myself next time." Sean stood and pulled Jaime with him to the bedroom.

"I didn't mean to mislead you with breakfast," Jaime said after Sean closed the door behind them.

"It was stupid. You didn't really do anything." He should have noticed Aleksandra didn't seem to think it was special at all.

"Maybe not, but I did just cook a late dinner from scratch for your friends, and I think it's pretty obvious that I did that just for you," Jaime said as he backed Sean against the bedroom door. He brushed his fingers under the hem of Sean's shirt as he bent down to brush his lips over the base of Sean's neck. "And I took the train here just to see you even after Alana took over our date, so I wasn't even sure I was going to get laid for my trouble."

"You're really going to get laid," Sean mumbled as Jaime pushed his shirt up and over his head. "I had the plan to promise you sex because it's been too long."

"Not letting that happen again." Jaime threw off his own shirt before pulling Sean away from the door and pushing him to the bed. Sean held on instead of giving up his grip on Jaime's arms, pulling Jaime on top of him as Jaime's lips found his again. Jaime's kisses were light and hesitant until Sean palmed the back of his head and dragged him closer. Sean slid his tongue along Jaime's lips until Jaime let him in, but his hands tangled in Sean's hair instead of traveling south to push at his jeans.

"What's wrong?" Sean broke away just enough to whisper the words against Jaime's lips.

"Nothing." Jaime moved to kiss down his neck and then back up to suck behind his ear. Sean moaned as Jaime's teeth scraped against his skin before he soothed over the spot with his tongue. Sean was about to point out that Jaime wasn't known for taking so long when Jaime whispered against his ear. "What do you want?"

"Fuck me." Sean knew his voice was rough, but it got the reaction he was hoping for as Jaime's hips bucked against him.

"Sean." Jaime groaned, pausing to press his face against Sean's neck. Sean could feel him taking a deep breath to calm himself. That was the last thing Sean wanted. Sean stilled for a minute before running his hand over the back of Jaime's head and lifting his chin so their eyes met. Jaime's eyes were dilated with lust, but there was doubt he wasn't used to seeing.

"Are you freaking out on me?" Sean asked.

"No."

"Maybe a little?" Sean asked when Jaime didn't elaborate.

Jaime chuckled and tried to look away, but Sean cupped his cheek to hold him in place.

"Maybe a little," Jaime said. "But not enough that you need to give me an option to stop or anything."

"Okay." Sean held his gaze for a second more before pulling him into a slow kiss. Sean let his mouth fall open as Jaime deepened the kiss and pressed Sean into the mattress as he set the pace, and Sean relaxed in the slow build of lust. Jaime pulled away to let his lips travel over Sean's collarbone to his shoulder as he smoothed his hand down Sean's side.

When he finally moved to unbutton Sean's jeans, Sean only hesitated a second before reciprocating. Their hands bumped in the tight space, and Jaime let out a short laugh before sitting back on his heels to undo his own jeans and toss them aside with his boxers before stripping Sean as well.

Jaime's cock slid against his as Jaime dropped down and pressed their bodies flush against each other while he left little nips on Sean's throat. In all the times they'd had sex, it had never had this slow build, with Jaime pressed so close to him that Sean wasn't sure if it was the weight making it hard to breathe or something else.

When Jaime trailed his hand down his ass to pull on his leg, Sean went with the movement, bringing his leg up to wrap round Jaime and keep him close. Jaime stroked up and down his thigh before letting his fingers skim in the cleft of his ass.

"Fuck. Please." Sean used the slight bit of leverage he had to push up closer, letting out harsh short breaths as his cock slid over the thin layer of sweat between them. He felt the light press of Jaime's fingers against him before Jaime eased out of his grip enough to reach his night stand and pull the drawer open.

Sean couldn't even think to try and make out the words Jaime was whispering into his neck in between bites and kisses as Jaime's fingers teased and stroked inside of him, sending shocks through his body as Jaime soothed him with long, firm strokes down his side with his other hand.

He was shaking, and his brain was fighting for enough focus to beg when Jaime moved back enough to slide on a condom and pull Sean's leg up to give him room. Their eyes locked as Jaime slid inside him, and Sean held his gaze until his brain went fuzzy, and he pressed his head back against the pillow. Jaime took advantage of Sean's flexibility and pushed close against him as he set a pace of slow, deep thrusts that made something in Sean's chest clench

"Kiss me," Jaime said, close enough that Sean could feel the hot breath on his lips, and he tilted his head up. Jaime reached between them to wrap his hand around Sean's cock, and it was more of wet mix of hot air and tongue as they struggled to breathe between kisses. Sean pulled back just enough to stop himself from biting down on Jaime's lip as he came. Jaime buried his head in Sean's neck as he gave up control in quick thrusts before collapsing on Sean with a mixture of exhaustion and bliss.

It may have been seconds or minutes before Sean could think enough to speak, and even then he struggled against a stronger urge to sleep.

"That was amazing. So amazing that I'm going to fall asleep with you still on top of me if you let me."

"Are you going to complain about the mess in the morning if I let you?" Jaime mumbled.

"Probably."

Jaime groaned, but he rolled off him and wiped them off so that they wouldn't wake up to a sticky mess. He pushed at Sean's side until he moved enough for Jaime to straighten out the blankets before sliding in to spoon behind him. Sean took the hand resting on his stomach and pulled it up to hold close to his chest before drifting off.

SEAN WAS only beginning to gain consciousness to the pressure of kisses on his back and shoulders when he jerked awake to Travis yelling through the door. He groaned and curled into Jaime's chest without answering.

"Sorry. I didn't wake up early enough," Jaime said, even though he was awake enough to laugh at Sean's misery.

"Alana's still here," Travis called through the door.

"I hate you," Sean called back.

"I think that means you're supposed to get up," Jaime said when Sean didn't move.

"Lupe and Michael aren't working the last show today. You could come." Sean had thought of it when Travis said he'd decided to let them take an extra class for the next week instead. It was possible Jaime didn't want to see a show he'd already seen the week before, but he couldn't help being greedy for more time.

"You don't think anyone would notice me?" Jaime asked.

"You'll be in the balcony this late anyway. I can meet you somewhere else after the show. Unless you just need to get back."

"I don't. I can take the later train. We could do something after." Jaime pressed a kiss to his forehead, so maybe Sean wasn't alone in wanting more time. "But you should get up before they decide you're taking too long."

"Are you going to hide in here until I'm out of the bathroom?" Sean asked when Jaime made no move to get up after him.

"Just for the first ten minutes."

Sean nodded and slipped out the door. Alana whistled at him as he walked to the bathroom, and he couldn't even find it in him to be annoyed as he turned on the shower.

Jaime was sitting at the bar when he emerged from the bathroom. He didn't have the shell-shocked look he'd had the week before, but he still didn't look awake enough for whatever Alana was excited about.

"Jaime has never seen the whale," Alana said before Sean could even take the other stool next to Jaime.

"You've never seen the whale?" Sean asked.

"I'm still confused. Is this a real whale?" Jaime asked as he stood up.

"It's not a real whale. It's at the Natural History Museum," Sean said.

"You should go after the show. You'll still have time." Alana could be a hazard to his relationship, but she could also suggest the best dates so he didn't have to.

"To the Natural History Museum?" Jaime looked from Alana to Sean.

"Don't worry. You don't have to do the whole museum. Sean's scared of just about every other room in the whole building." And *that* was why Alana was a hazard.

"NO ENTOURAGE?" Jaime asked when met him at the subway station after the show.

"Travis is too cool for the whale unless he's dating a girl who thinks it's romantic. Alana has made me look bad enough for at least a week."

"How is a fake whale in a museum romantic?" Jaime asked as they crowded onto the train. It wasn't a packed car, but all the seats were taken. Sean leaned against Jaime instead of holding on to one of the poles, and fought a smile as Jaime wrapped an arm around his waist. "Is this somewhere you take all your dates?"

"No. I mostly go with Alana after class. It's relaxing. We just have to make sure we don't both fall asleep on the same day."

"You fall asleep?"

"Not often." Sean led the way out of the station, grabbing Jaime's hand when he tried to go in the subway entrance to the museum.

"Why are we going into the cold?"

"The Seventy-Seventh Street door is better."

"Was Alana serious about you being scared of the other rooms?" There was amusement in Jaime's tone, but he adjusted his hand to thread his fingers through Sean's as he said it.

"I'm not scared of them. I just think stuffed animals that used to be alive are weird." He could handle them if he had to, but it felt like their dead, glassy eyes were judging him.

"And this door doesn't have them?"

"It has the least and they're easy to ignore," Sean admitted as he led them into the main hall.

"Wow, I can see why you like it." Jaime's gaze traveled around the room as they descended to the main floor of the hall, and Sean pulled them to where a few people were already laying on the floor.

"You want me to lie on the floor of a public museum?" Jaime asked when Sean sat down and tried to pull him down after him.

"Yes. That's kind of the point." Sean tugged at his hand again, and Jaime at least sat down next to him. Sean lay down, admiring the way the dim blue light illuminated Jaime's face. "Come on. Do you want me to tell Alana we came all the way over here, and you refused to lie down?"

"I don't think you're supposed to threaten your dates," Jaime grumbled, but he finally stretched out on his back next to Sean, and he didn't object when Sean moved closer to use his shoulder as a pillow.

"Worth seeing?" Sean asked after a few minutes of watching the shifting blue-and-white waves inside the glass ceiling above them.

"Yeah. Worth seeing."

CHAPTER 12

THE FOLLOWING week, classes were as relaxed as they'd ever been before ending early on the Wednesday before Thanksgiving. Sean had to leave without an airport good-bye because Jaime had one last class, but the good-bye he got for going to the train station with Jaime Wednesday morning was worth it. As much as part of him wanted to spend his days off in Jaime's bed, he hadn't seen his parents or his sister since they'd visited in the summer. Travis used to say it was a waste of money to travel for Thanksgiving when he'd also go back to California for Christmas, but he'd given up on that once he'd actually met Sean's mom.

In California. My plane didn't crash.

He sent the same text to Travis and Jaime before adding, *San Francisco is almost as cold as NY. But I'll have to sleep alone. :(,* in a separate text to Jaime.

Travis texted back, *Learn to use your phone before you start sexting or I'm forwarding to Alana.*

It was probably just as well that he had to get his carry-on from the overhead bin and get off the plane instead of texting Travis back. No one had ever picked up his bag from the baggage carousel to steal it, but he always thought one day it would happen.

He found his dad in the crowd before he even had to call. Flying home for holidays since he left for boarding school when he was fourteen meant they had a system down. But years of living away from home didn't lessen the way it felt to have his dad wrap him in a hug after months away. BART was packed with people, but the trains emptied as they approached the east bay, and the parking lot at the station closest to his parents' house was empty enough that his sister could pull up to the curb to meet them without a long wait.

"It's Thanksgiving, not Christmas," Elizabeth called out the window as their dad loaded his suitcase into the truck. "You're here for three days. How do you even need a suitcase?"

"I brought presents."

"You're the reason my kids think Thanksgiving is the same as Christmas. Zach's kindergarten teacher thinks he's confused because he was excited to get presents on Thanksgiving. I'm blaming you if he gets held back."

"His teacher is jealous Zach has a cooler uncle than she does," Sean said. Elizabeth could complain all she wanted. Sean only got to see his niece and nephew four or five times a year. It was his job as an uncle to give them presents every time he saw them so they'd never decide they had better things to do than hang out with him. It was a show of how well he was doing that Zach ran out the door of his parents' house as soon as they pulled up, and didn't complain that he was too old for Sean to pick him up and carry him.

"Mrs. Rivera said toys are for Christmas, but she's wrong, right?" Zach asked.

"She's right. Your uncle is just confused," Elizabeth said before he could answer.

"Then I want to be confused too," Zach said with as serious of an expression a five-year-old could have.

Sean laughed, carrying Zach inside the house while his dad followed with his suitcase. Zach's sister Jenny gazed at him with wide eyes from where she was stacking blocks on the living room floor with Elizabeth's husband. She'd just turned one when Elizabeth and Eric had brought the kids to New York in June, and it had taken her two days to stop being afraid of Sean then.

"Hey. Remember me?" Sean sat down on the floor next to Eric and picked up a block to stack on her tower. She watched him for a few seconds before handing him another block and pointing out where it should go.

"When you have your own, I'm buying them all the noisy toys," Elizabeth said, but she was smiling as she sat on the couch as his mom came in from the kitchen. His mom leaned down to kiss the top of Sean's head before sitting next to Elizabeth on the couch.

"You'll have to fight Travis for the job."

"There's plenty to go around. We can work together." Elizabeth rolled her eyes when Sean took a break from playing with Jenny's blocks to open his suitcase and pull out the tablet he'd brought for Zach. She shouldn't complain. It was educational. It was supposed to help kids learn Spanish. If he'd tested it out a bit, it was just because he'd learned that, at this age, it was better to open things and put in batteries in advance.

"I don't even have to ask where the inspiration for that one came from," Elizabeth said as Zach started trying to figure out everything the toy did. "Do you at least have some pictures? I tried e-mailing Travis about him, but he was as unhelpful as ever."

"I don't have a lot." For someone who took pictures, Jaime never seemed to want to be in them or take any of himself, but Aleksandra had sent one in the last week that Sean might have set as the background image on his phone. He handed his phone to Elizabeth so she could look.

"So, tall, dark, and handsome?" she said, tilting the phone so their mom could look. "I'd say it's not your normal type, except I think your type is actually just any guy who is attractive."

His phone buzzed as she started to hand it back, and he grabbed it before she could pull it back to get a look at the text.

I checked the weather. It's much colder here. But my bed would be a lot hotter with you in it.

"And you're going to be like this all weekend," Elizabeth said when he ignored her to type back.

You can't send me things like that when I'm playing with blocks with a one-year-old. But later....

Then text me when you're in bed.

It was hours before Sean broke away from his family to go to his room upstairs. He felt like a zombie as he stripped to his underwear and climbed in bed. Getting up for one last class in the morning, combined with the time difference and chasing around two small children, had the text blurring on his phone as he typed.

Finally in bed. Are you still up? Can I call?

His phone started ringing instead, and he turned on his side in the dark as he held the phone to his ear.

"Hey. I was just about to sleep," Jaime whispered. "I think Lupe's already asleep in the living room, though."

"Sorry. My family forgets it's still two a.m. for me."

"Does that mean you'll wake up at a normal time for them?" Jaime asked, the amusement clear in his voice.

"I don't like to set unrealistic expectations for the future."

Jaime's laugh made him wish Jaime was spooned behind him instead of across the country, although they only managed to share a bed once a week most of the time. It seemed easier when Jaime was only an hour away and Sean had the option to go over if he really wanted.

"Elizabeth said to tell you she's impressed I'm dating someone smart for once. She also says you're hot, so it's probably not that I got better taste and more that I got really lucky."

"You told your family about me?" Jaime asked.

"They asked. Is that bad?" Sean was smart enough to not tell Jaime how many questions his parents has asked about Jaime's plans after he graduated, but he'd thought Elizabeth's comments were safe enough.

"No, it's fine."

"Is Lupe staying all weekend?" Sean asked.

"Just Thanksgiving and the day after, so she can make me feed her. She's leaving Saturday morning," Jaime said, and then paused for moment before adding, "so you could come over after your flight gets in—if you're not too tired from the trip."

"If I am, can I just sleep in your bed?" Sean was going to blame his exhaustion if Jaime decided it was weird for him to just show up to sleep in Jaime's bed.

"Yeah," Jaime said after a silence that stretched a little long. "Yeah. That's fine. You get back around two, right?"

"Yeah. I should drop some stuff off at home, but then I can come over."

"Good. You should sleep. You're tired, and I have to get up early to cook," Jaime said.

"I can't believe you're cooking a whole Thanksgiving dinner yourself." Sean always went home, but even Travis went to Steph's house instead of cooking for himself.

"It keeps Lupe from being too homesick."

"That's good. I'll call you tomorrow night?"

"Yeah. Now go to sleep. I'm going to laugh if your nephew wakes you up early."

Sean agreed to sleep, but he let Jaime be the one to hang up after they said good night.

CHAPTER 13

BACK IN NY! I'll text you when I know what train I'm on. :)

Sean was pretty sure all his friends and Jaime would argue against him taking a cab from the airport instead of the subway, but if he wanted to be lazy about dropping his stuff off at home before taking another cab to Grand Central, he was allowed to splurge.

"You're not even staying, are you?" Alana asked as soon as he stepped in the door.

"I'll be back tomorrow," Sean called as he walked past to leave his suitcase in his room and change into something that didn't smell like he'd been stuck on an airplane for hours.

"Just remember you have class Monday morning," Travis said as he walked back out the door a minute later.

The train ride seemed longer than normal. He'd been up early to get to the airport, and he'd never been able to sleep on planes. He was just tired enough to be miserable and not tired enough to fall asleep sitting up on the train. Maybe Jaime would have pity for him and curl up around him in bed, even if Sean was the only one who was tired.

Sean leaned against Jaime as soon as he found him in the station at White Plains. He was too tired to care if Jaime thought it was weird that he just walked up and buried his face in Jaime's neck as he wrapped his arms around his waist. Jaime let out a short laugh as his arms went around Sean's back and held him close.

"Come on. Ten minutes in my car and then I promise you can sleep in my bed." Jaime pulled back, but he kept his arm around Sean's shoulder and let Sean lean against him as they walked to the car. Sean closed his eyes for just a second as Jaime started the car, and the next thing he knew, Jaime was shaking his shoulder.

"You couldn't sleep on the plane or the train over here, but you can doze off the second you're with me. I should be offended," Jaime said, but he couldn't be too offended because he was still stroking through Sean's hair.

"I sleep better with you," Sean mumbled, still too asleep to think about what he was saying.

"Yeah," Jaime said, pressing a kiss to Sean's temple. "But it's better inside. In the bed. And I'm not carrying you up the stairs, so you have to wake up and walk there."

Then Jaime was gone. He got out and walked around to open Sean's door to pull at him until Sean got up and stepped into the cold. The wind whipping against his cheeks jolted him awake and he cursed, but it gave him the energy to follow Jaime up the stairs and into the warm apartment.

Aleksandra was on the phone, but she waved as they walked past on the way to the bedroom. They'd just stepped inside when there were loud knocks on the front door.

"Lie down," Jaime said. "It's probably the Mormon guys that live upstairs. I keep trying to just tell them we're not interested in a nice way, but I think that's making it worse. Maybe I should just go ahead and admit I'm gay."

Sean had unbuttoned his shirt and started push off his jeans when he heard a loud mix of Spanish outside. It was too fast for him to even pick out any of the common words he knew. He pulled his jeans back up, not stopping to think past worrying about how upset Jaime sounded before opening the door to the bedroom. He swung the door open just a second before he recognized the female voice and realized he should have stayed hidden.

Aleksandra moved to step in front of him, but Lupe was already staring at him with his hair messed up from Jaime running his fingers through it to wake him up and his shirt still hanging open. There was silence as time seem to freeze on him before Lupe turned back to Jaime and started yelling in Spanish all over again, and Sean jolted into action, buttoning up his shirt as though that would make anything better. He looked at Aleksandra, hoping she could give him some idea of what they were saying besides Lupe saying his name multiple times, but she looked as lost as he was. Either way, he couldn't let Jaime deal with how badly Lupe was taking his presence alone.

"Lupe." Sean said her name as he stepped toward them, and she turned to look at him again.

"Don't talk to me. You don't want to talk to me," she snapped, so much stronger than the eager student he was used to seeing at the studio.

"If you let me explain," Sean started.

"Sean, don't," Jaime said, stepping between them as Lupe spoke over him.

"You don't need to explain," Lupe said. "I can figure it out. What I can't figure out is why you thought it was appropriate to fuck up my cousin's life. You want to be how you are, that's fine. I don't care. I didn't care, but he has a family."

"I'm not trying to mess that up." It wasn't like he had some kind of awful plan to take Jaime away from her.

"Well, you are," Lupe snapped, just as Jaime said, "Stop. Leave him out of this."

Jaime turned to Aleksandra, not even looking at him as he said, "Lexi, can you take my car and take him home? Please."

Sean stepped toward him, but Jaime backed away.

"Sean, just go. Let her take you home."

He wanted to say something. He wanted ask Jaime to call him and let him know if he was okay. He wanted to ask if he was even going to hear from Jaime again, but Jaime turned away from him.

"Come on." Aleksandra touched his elbow, pulling him enough to make him move with her past Lupe to where he'd left his boots by the door. The seconds of silence it took for them to both get their shoes on and grab their coats felt like forever, but nothing was as bad as the way Jaime turned his head away when Sean tried to look at him before they went outside.

"I'm taking you to the station. I know he said to take you home, but you can't really want me to leave him alone for that long," Aleksandra said, rushing to the car now that they were outside.

"I don't," Sean said as she pulled out of the parking lot. "I don't want to leave him either."

"I know." She sighed and turned toward him for a second when they stopped at the intersection. "But I don't think we can really argue with him about that on top of everything."

"I can wait at the station and come back if he wants me to."

"Sean, probably not tonight, but I'll try to get him to call you. I promise."

"Thanks." Sean was silent for a minute before he couldn't help adding, "If he won't, can you just text me and let me know how he is?"

"He'll probably ask me not to," she said, but then added, "I'll text you something if I can."

The rest of the ride was quiet until they pulled up to the station he'd only just left. He was reaching for the door when she took his wrist to stop him.

"If he doesn't call and doesn't talk to you right away, don't give up on him. Please don't give up on him."

"I won't, and I'll come back tonight if he changes his mind. At any time." It might cost a lot to come back in the middle of the night if he had to, but how could he not do it when everything felt like his fault?

Sean let the first few trains leave without him. He told himself he'd wait an hour. Then he let himself wait two hours. After three hours without a call or a text, he had to face the reality that he should go home. He was still tired, but now he wasn't sure he could sleep at all.

Alana was sitting at the kitchen counter watching Travis cook when he came into the apartment. She opened her mouth to say something, but stopped when she looked at him. Sean stumbled to the couch and she met him there, sitting close to him and resting her head on his shoulder.

"Do we have to kill him?"

"No. It's not his fault." The last thing Jaime needed was for Alana to make things worse.

"Do you want to be more specific?" Travis asked as he came to sit on Sean's other side.

"Lupe caught us."

They sat for a minute soaking in the situation.

"She didn't like, *see* anything, though, did she? I mean, you weren't naked or anything, right?" Alana asked.

"No. Seriously? What's wrong with you?"

"I don't know! I was just trying to assess the damage! So she just saw you together and she was smart enough to draw the right conclusion."

"I think? I don't even know. We went in, she knocked, and Jaime went to get it. Then there was just a lot of yelling that I didn't understand. I tried to talk to her, but she just yelled at me." Sean leaned forward to put his head in his hands. "Then he told me to leave."

"He just kicked you out?" Travis said.

"No. He told Aleksandra to drive me home, and she drove me to the station because she didn't want to leave for a long time. I sat there for a while in case he wanted me to come back, but he didn't call or text or anything." His eyes were watering, but he ignored it as he pulled out his phone. The battery was dying from how much he'd kept checking it, as if he wouldn't have noticed it ringing or vibrating. "I should plug in my phone. In case he calls."

"I'll get it." Alana went to where he'd dropped his messenger bag by the door and pulled out his charger. She plugged it in by the TV so the cord could stretch to the coffee table where he could still see it.

"Have you eaten since lunch?" Travis asked.

"I can't eat."

"You can eat something small. I was making soup anyway." Travis kept talking as he walked to the kitchen. "You need to eat and take care of yourself, or you'll make yourself sick. You can't help him if you don't eat."

"What if he doesn't call?" Sean took the bowl of soup from Travis but set it on the coffee table instead of trying it.

"Give him some time before you worry about that."

"You're telling me to give him time? You don't even like him."

"I don't hate him. I just thought this was a bad idea because this could happen. You're lucky, and your parents are amazing, but I've worked with a lot of dancers who weren't so lucky, especially dancing in Texas in high school. Lupe might be okay. She knows you. She has at least one other gay friend. But it might take some time."

"She said it was my fault. That I was fucking up his life and his family."

"It's not your fault. You know that. Jaime knows that. You never made him do anything," Alana said. She picked up the bowl from the table and put it back in his hands. "Drink half, and I'll drink the rest."

Sean expected one of them to fight him when he handed the bowl back with a bit more than half left, but Travis let it go and didn't even complain when Alana turned on the TV to the same awful movie Sean had laughed at with her last week.

He was dozing off on Travis's shoulder when his phone buzzed and jolted him awake. If he'd jumped for his phone any other day, Alana would have laughed at him, but now she just put her hand on his knee in a small gesture of comfort.

It was Aleksandra and not Jaime.

Sorry it's late. I wanted to get Jaime to approve of me texting you because that seemed better. He's not really okay and Lupe is very upset. They argued for a while, but she did agree not to tell the rest of his family for now. He doesn't want to talk to you yet.

Sean waited a few seconds, hoping there was more before he gave in and replied.

How did she know? Did she just happen to be there when we got in?

Somehow he knew it wasn't that simple. She'd never been there before. She never stopped by without warning. When Jaime had talked to him the night before, he'd mentioned knowing Lupe had plans. When Aleksandra took a few minutes to answer, he knew it wasn't good.

One of the other dancers saw him at your show last week. She mentioned it to Lupe in class. I guess there have been rumors you were dating someone, and she planted the idea. Then she noticed Jaime texting and calling someone while she was here. She heard him say something about Saturday afternoon and waited.

Jaime had asked him if it was safe, and Sean had told him no one would notice. Aleksandra sent another text before he could think of a reply.

I don't think he really blames you. I told him that dating you was risky in the beginning and he did it anyway. He's just really overwhelmed right now. Get some rest. We all need sleep now. I'll work on getting him to call you tomorrow. If he won't, I'll at least let you know.

Sean typed back a simple *Thanks* before putting his phone back on the table.

"It's my fault." He hadn't even had to ask her if Jaime blamed him. She wouldn't have brought it up if it wasn't at all true.

"Did he say that?" Alana asked.

"No. It wasn't even him. He didn't want to text me. It was Aleksandra. She didn't say it either, but it is."

"Can we just read?" Travis asked before Alana could ask another question and Sean handed him the phone. Travis scrolled through the texts before passing it to Alana. Any other time, Alana would have taken advantage of having his unlocked phone to scroll through all his texts with Jaime, but now she set it on the table after only a few seconds.

"She didn't say it was your fault," Travis said.

"She said that 'he didn't really blame me,' which means he said he blamed me. He should. He asked if anyone would notice if he was there. I told him they wouldn't. I told him it would be okay."

"And he still knew the risks as much as you did. He always knew," Travis reminded him.

"You told me and I didn't listen." Sean knew he hadn't even tried to listen.

"I didn't really expect you to listen. You liked him, and obviously he cares about you because he took a lot of chances. I'm sure he knew what could happen. Either way, you didn't do this. You didn't force him to do anything. He was gay long before he met you. It probably would have happened eventually." Travis stood and pulled him to his feet. "She's right that you should sleep, though."

"I'm not going to be able to sleep." He was supposed to be with Jaime, in Jaime's bed, with Jaime wrapped around him.

"Yeah, you will." Travis pushed him toward the bedroom. He started to argue that he needed his phone, but when he turned around, Alana was already unplugging it and walking past him with it to the bedroom.

"I made all your ringers so loud they'll wake up the whole apartment. If you don't wake up and he calls, I'll wake you up." Alana set the phone on the bedside table and climbed in the bed ahead of him.

Sean nodded. Even changing into pajama pants felt like work. Alana wasn't Jaime, but it was better than sleeping alone. The exhaustion pulled him into sleep within minutes.

WHEN HE woke, Alana was sitting up next to him reading a book and it was already almost eleven o'clock.

"Sorry. No calls or messages," she said as soon she noticed he was awake. "It's early, though. You're normally still asleep at noon on a Sunday."

"Should I try texting him?" He wasn't sure what he could say that would mean anything. They hadn't even said "I love you" yet. He hadn't been sure he was there. He tended to fall fast instead of slow, but it was probably a sign now that he cared more about Jaime being okay than he cared about feeling better himself. But he wasn't going to tell Jaime that through text—not when he'd gone to the trouble to learn the words in Spanish in case Jaime said it in Spanish first, and he hadn't heard anything that sounded similar in the Spanish Jaime had whispered into his skin.

"It's early. Give it a little more time. I'm sure he knows you want to talk to him. Aleksandra told him."

"What if he never wants to talk to me?" He reached past her to pick up his phone and scroll through the contacts. He couldn't help hovering over Jaime's name before dropping the phone back on the bed.

"I'm going to beat Travis to telling you that's overdramatic. Please don't say that to him, or he'll drag us into the studio because he thinks you need a distraction." Alana slid out of bed and walked to the door. "I'm telling Travis you're awake, so you probably want to get out here."

He made it through Sunday with Alana trying to distract him until she had to make an appearance at her house. On Monday, he plowed through every class and checked his phone during every break, but there wasn't even a message from Aleksandra.

"I can't take your modern class tomorrow." He was supposed to be helping Travis choreograph a piece for the next season, but Sean was pretty sure he was just a distraction.

"Like hell." Travis threw him a glare before turning back to what he was writing down. "You're going to that class."

"Lupe is taking that class, unless she skips. She only has one more week before you sign off on her evaluation. She's not going to skip."

"Yeah? Okay, then. How's she's gonna get there?"

"I have to skip your class."

"So you can do what?" Travis dropped his pen to give Sean his full attention. "Chase his car down the street if he's here? I'm not letting you do that. I will handcuff you to the barre. He might not even be there, and if he is and he doesn't want to see you, chasing him down the street isn't going to help."

"That idea sounded better in my head."

"I'm going to handcuff you to Alana when I have to teach the lower levels. We'll call it a team-building exercise."

"Why do you have handcuffs?"

CHAPTER 14

SEAN KNEW he was driving Alana crazy. He'd been distracted in every class and missed so many cues that she'd declared she wasn't letting him do a single lift with her all day. By the time they were stretching before Travis's class, he was alternating between watching the door for Lupe and looking out the window. It didn't face any street Jaime would drive down, but he kept looking anyway.

"Stop. Stretch with me. Even you agree that chasing after his car isn't a good idea," Alana whispered.

"I don't want to see her." He'd always liked Lupe. She was only a few months younger than Alana, but between Jaime's habit of calling Lupe and Michael "the kids" and Alana having more street smarts than Travis, he only remembered Alana's age when Travis mentioned an old TV show and she gave them a blank look. Lupe had always felt like this kid who thought they hung the stars. Now all he could hear was the way she'd said "how he was" was fine if he didn't ruin Jaime's life.

"You know Travis. He will be professional and still keep her as far as possible from you the entire class."

"And forgive me if I freak out and leave," Sean said.

"Yes, but he'll still make you make up the entire class later, and he'll make me make up the class after I go after you, even though he'd want me to go after you. So please don't do that to me." Alana rolled her eyes when he jumped for the third time to the studio door opening behind them. "Stop. I'll just tell you when it's her so you don't freak out every time."

A few minutes later, he could tell by the expression on Alana's face that it was Lupe who had come through the door.

"Well, that's weird. Michael's not with her," Alana whispered.

Travis called for them to start before he could answer. Lupe must have lingered in the dressing room so she could enter right on time.

They were five minutes into class when Michael came in, and it was as if the entire small company stopped breathing. There were limited excuses for being late or absent from Travis's classes, and almost all of them involved someone being in the hospital.

"Continue the combination," Travis said, as if any of them had dared to stop.

Sean couldn't hear whatever excuse Michael gave, but whatever it was made Travis pause, and Michael joined a line in the back of the class.

Alana must have had a death wish, because she pulled Sean toward Michael when they were waiting for the other half of the class to finish a combination.

"Why were you late?" Alana whispered.

Michael glanced at Travis, who was correcting another dancer's form.

"Lupe told me what happened. I tried talking to her, and after that mess, I didn't want to get in a car with her, so I took the train." Michael glanced back at Travis before he finished talking to the other dancer. "I got confused on the subway. Aleksandra drove her. Jaime's still worried about her even after everything."

Travis glared and didn't give them a chance to talk for the rest of class, but he kept Michael and Lupe after he dismissed the class. Sean wished for a second that Travis would bend his rules and let them leave instead of making up the time Michael missed, just so he could stop pretending Lupe wasn't keeping an unusual distance. He'd made it past them and all the way to the dressing room before realizing that if Lupe was held late, he'd have time to talk to Aleksandra outside.

Travis was going to kill him if he got sick from slipping on his shoes and running outside in just his dance pants and hoodie, but he'd already used up time, and Travis wouldn't keep them for more than a few minutes. Aleksandra was sitting in the driver's seat when he spotted the car, but she opened the door and stepped out when she saw him coming.

"He's not here. They're still fighting. She's not happy with me either, but you know he'd blame himself if she came on her own and something happened to her," Aleksandra said. "I told him nothing would happen to her, but he's an overprotective freak who thinks she's still twelve years old."

"I know. And I know if I really want to say something, I could text him, but I don't know if he'd read it, and I'm hoping if it goes through you, maybe he'll listen."

"Sean." Aleksandra sighed, then rolled her eyes when the wind whipped around him and he shivered. "What's wrong with you? Right now all I'm going to tell him is you're an idiot who is going to get pneumonia."

"Can you just tell him—"

Sean paused. He hadn't actually thought up anything to say. He didn't know what Jaime would even want him to say. "Can you tell him I'll do whatever he wants? If he wants to see me, and he doesn't want to talk about it, I can do that. I can come there, or he can come over. Or he can just text me and tell me anything I can do."

"I'll tell him, but you should go." Aleksandra nodded behind him, and he turned to see Lupe walking toward them. She'd stopped on the sidewalk, but when their eyes met, she started walking again.

He thought for a second that she was going to force him into a confrontation, but Travis turned the corner behind her and his strides were quick enough that he walked past her before she reached them.

"You're going to freeze to death." Travis glared at him and pushed his coat in his arms. Sean pulled on his coat, and didn't resist when Travis took his elbow to pull him past Lupe back toward the studio.

"You're not wearing a coat either," Sean said as they stepped back into the heat.

"And whose fault is that? Alana only had time to bring me yours when she realized you ran outside like a lunatic."

"I had to try."

"I know, but I'm not letting you get on a train so you can bang down his door, so you might as well get your stuff to go home. Alana went with Michael so he doesn't end up in Harlem instead of Grand Central."

"Are you going to put that he was late on his evaluation?" Sean was almost sure he knew the answer.

"He gets one pass for telling Lupe off."

IT WAS seven thirty when Sean's phone buzzed. He jumped for it, and Travis didn't bother to comment from where he was making a stir-fry in the kitchen. Alana had taken pity on him and was only texting them on Travis's phone, so it was worth jumping for.

It was Jaime.

I'm sorry I didn't text earlier. I just don't really want to talk about it. Can I come over anyway?

Sean didn't hesitate to text back, *Of course. Whatever you want.*

Ok. I'll come over. Is everyone there?

"Jaime wants to come over," Sean said before texting back. "Can you kind of hide in your room?"

"Yeah. Just don't try to cook for him to make him feel better. I'll leave you some food or something."

No. Alana is at her actual home. Travis said he'd give us space.

Jaime didn't answer for a few minutes.

Thanks. I'm getting on the train.

The time crawled after Travis showered and disappeared into his room. Sean texted Alana for a distraction and that helped a little, even if she told him he was an idiot and that changing out of sweatpants when he wasn't leaving the apartment was stupid.

Alana was trying to distract him with tales of the three different guys her sister was dating when there was a soft knock on the door. He tossed his phone aside. She'd understand if he didn't answer her anymore.

When Sean opened the door, Jaime was studying the floor, and his hands were hidden in the pockets of his leather jacket. He looked up at Sean through his eyelashes like he thought Sean was going to be mad at him for not calling, instead of just being worried about him. If he had been mad, it would have vanished with the way Jaime's eyes darted away again as he shifted on his feet.

"Hey, come in." Sean took his wrist to tug him inside, and reached behind him to push the door closed. He let his hand skim up the smooth leather jacket to curl around the back of Jaime's neck. When he pulled the taller man to him, Jaime came easily, wrapping his arms around Sean's waist as Sean held him.

"I'm sorry. I should have texted or called," Jaime said, his lips brushing over Sean's neck with each word.

"I'm not mad. Really worried. Not mad."

Jaime shook his head without actually moving away.

"Is this what it feels like when your parents say they aren't mad, just really disappointed? Because my mom is always just fine being mad, so I've never gotten the concept, but this feels like the same idea."

Sean couldn't help letting out a short laugh of relief. If Jaime could joke even a little, he probably wasn't going to break up with Sean because Lupe wanted him to.

"Maybe. My parents are champions at that one. *Travis* is a champion at that one already. I fear for his future children. But that's not really what I was going for." Sean tried to pull away to get a better look at his face, but when Jaime resisted, he gave up. "Are you hungry? There's food."

"I ate." Jaime sighed against him. "Sorry. It's probably weird that I just want to stand here."

"No. It's fine." Sean let his hand stroke over Jaime's back. "We might want to move to the bed at some point, though. Standing might get difficult if we do this for hours."

Jaime nodded into his neck, but he didn't pull away, so Sean held him tighter and pressed a kiss to the side of his head where he could reach. After a few minutes, Jaime took a deep breath and pulled away.

"Bed?" Sean asked.

"Yeah," Jaime agreed, walking around him toward the bedroom.

He didn't bother to turn on the light, so Sean didn't either. He just watched in the sliver of light from the street that peeked through his curtains as Jaime slipped his jeans off and left them in a pile on the floor before pulling back the covers and climbing into Sean's bed. Sean followed suit and slipped in next to him, but Jaime didn't move toward him immediately like he'd expected. Instead he lay on his side facing Sean.

"I don't even know what's going on," Jaime whispered after a few seconds of silence. "She said she wouldn't tell anyone, but I think she just meant she wouldn't tell anyone yet."

"You don't think it'll be okay?"

"I know it won't be," Jaime said. Sean was still trying to think up the perfect response when Jaime spoke again. "I asked once. When I was seventeen. Lupe was in a production, and the director was gay. Her mom almost made her pull out, but Lupe argued that she had to learn to be around people she didn't agree with. I didn't think Lupe really meant anything by it. She just wanted to dance. But after my mom met her director at the show, she said it was a shame that he'd hurt his mother like that. So I asked. Sort of. I asked if she'd disown my brother if he was gay and she said, 'Of course.' She didn't even have to think about it."

There wasn't a thing Sean could say to that. If comforting words existed that would help, he had no idea what they were, so he gave up and just moved closer to Jaime instead. He took Jaime's hand, and Jaime let himself be pulled so his head was pillowed on Sean's chest.

"How do you make me talk about shit I don't want to talk about?" Jaime mumbled into his chest.

"I don't know. I kind of thought I was going to have to force myself not to ask questions while you didn't say anything." Sean squeezed the arm he had around Jaime's shoulders. "Maybe you did want to talk about it?"

"No. I don't," Jaime said, "but maybe I wanted you to know."

WHEN TRAVIS yelled through the door eight thirty, Sean opened his eyes to find Jaime still waking up in front of him.

"Why is he waking you up so early?" Jaime asked. "It's early, right?"

"Company classes start at ten. I haven't convinced Steph or Travis that's too early. They claim they need the afternoons to teach the lower-level classes that kids pay to take after school. I tried to offer Steph money to move them later a long time ago, and Travis called me a spoiled rich brat." When Jaime gave him a strange look, Sean shrugged. "That was a week after we met. We weren't friends yet."

"So we should have slept earlier?"

"I'd rather be tired all day," Sean said as he sat up and stretched. When he looked in the mirror, he saw a small bruise at the base of his neck where Jaime had bitten down as he came, but it was already faint. Alana might notice it, but that would just be because she always noticed everything.

"And I can sleep on the train home so I don't fall asleep in class." Jaime pulled Sean back down on the bed after Sean yelled back at Travis's warning. "I still have projects to work on and turn in next week, but you can come over Friday or Saturday if you want."

"I will." Sean almost asked if Jaime was still going home the next week, but stopped himself. It didn't seem right to bring anything up when he had to leave. Even then, he couldn't help adding, "Let me know if you need me to come over sooner, okay? I can work it out. It's not that far."

"I'm fine," Jaime said, but Sean's doubt must have shown on his face because he added, "but I'll tell you. You don't need to run out in the cold to talk to Lexi when she brings Lupe for her final intern evaluation. Please tell me she made up the thing about you not even having a coat on."

"I had a sweatshirt."

"Travis is going to kill me if you get sick."

CHAPTER 15

JAIME KEPT up a steady stream of texts and calls, but it didn't escape Sean's notice that he never brought up Lupe or his family. It was all random complaints about the projects he had to turn in before the end of the semester while still finishing enough freelance work to make rent.

When Sean wandered from Jaime's bedroom into the living room of Jaime's apartment on Saturday afternoon, Jaime and Aleksandra were already awake and sitting on the floor with photographs spread around them.

"We saved you food," Jaime said, getting up when he noticed Sean standing behind him. "I didn't want to wake you up just to make you watch us work."

Sean followed him to the kitchen as Jaime pulled a plate out of the refrigerator and put it in the microwave. Sean considered pointing out that even he could use a microwave, but when he stepped behind Jaime and dropped a kiss on his shoulder, Jaime reached back to take Sean's hands and pull him closer so Sean was pressed against Jaime's back with his arms wrapped around his waist.

Sean didn't realize he was expecting a comment from Aleksandra about how nauseating they were until it didn't come, even after he'd snuggled closer and kissed the back of Jaime's neck. When he tilted his head behind him, she just dropped her head back down to the pictures in front of her. He was still trying to figure out how to take that when the microwave beeped and Jaime pushed him away so he could take the plate.

Sean followed him back to the array of photographs in the living room, sitting on the couch to eat while Jaime dropped back down to the floor in front of him.

"We have to pick fifteen that tell a common story for our final portfolio," Aleksandra explained. "Well, Jaime does. I picked mine already. The problem is that Jaime has an amazing series he did with my friend, and he's too scared to turn it in, so he's trying to pick between all of these. And they're good enough, but good enough doesn't work when you know you're holding back on amazing."

"What's yours?" Sean asked instead of jumping into the trap Aleksandra was trying to set. If the glares Jaime was sending her way were a sign, he might have better luck trying to bring it up again when they were alone. Then again, the groan that question got from Jaime told him that question was just as bad.

"Actually, she should show you. Please tell her she can't use her pictures and make her start over," Jaime said.

"He's not going to do that," Aleksandra said, but there was a break in her voice as she got up and went to her room. She came back and handed him a black portfolio. "Please don't make me start over. Jaime's not being fair. I'm better at movement and this professor likes emotional portraits. Jaime's going to get an A no matter what he decides to turn in. They're not going in a show or anything. It's just a final project."

Sean already had an idea of what he was going to see when he opened the cover, but it still felt odd to see pictures of himself he hadn't known were taken. Except, he had known, kind of. Jaime had mentioned that Aleksandra had taken pictures at the dress rehearsals, even though she wasn't supposed to do that. He hadn't thought much about the pictures beyond that he couldn't mind if all she used them for was to get Jaime to come back to him.

But somehow he'd thought she'd taken a bunch of pictures of him dancing. He was used to that. Most people weren't allowed to take pictures at rehearsals, because Steph hired people for that. She often let photographers in who were interested, and Alana had once done a series for a photographer who was doing a show focused on dancers who had grown up in the city. These pictures weren't like that. There were close-ups of him and Alana as they sat on the edge of the stage to listen to Travis's corrections. There was a shot of him with Travis after they'd finished one day. He'd let his mind drift to Jaime long enough that Travis had seen it on his face, and Travis had stopped the conversation he'd been having with Steph to come check on him.

There were pictures of Alana and him dancing Travis's piece, but even those seemed raw in a way that differed from the professional pictures Steph's photographer had taken—maybe because then he'd known her photographer was there.

"I know I should have asked. I wasn't planning to use them for anything but showing Jaime how stupid he was, but then they ended up being so good," Aleksandra said when he kept flipping back and forth instead of answering. "But if you really don't want me to use them, I'll find something else."

"No." Sean shook his head. It was weird seeing it like that, but there wasn't actually anything that made him look bad. "Well, you should probably get permission from Travis to use the ones from the dance. But if I say it's okay, he'll let you. He'll probably want copies, and then he'll make Steph hire you next time."

"Now you're just encouraging her," Jaime said, but he leaned back against Sean's leg and smiled up at him. "Can you at least let her take some where you look like I make you really happy, so I can stop feeling guilty about these?"

"Please," Aleksandra said before he could answer. "You could just take some yourself. Oh right, they are all over your phone anyway."

"I hate you," Jaime said, but he laughed from his space between Sean's legs.

"You love me, and I showed him my project and he said it's fine, so you could at least show him what your project should be. And I'm going to point out that Anastasia posed for those pictures, and she wants you to show them before you try to say they're exploitative. They aren't even nude. There's, like, maybe a side boob in one of them."

"That's not the point," Jaime said.

"No. It's not." Aleksandra looked up at Sean, but he'd already decided that staying out of her argument was a better idea than getting dragged into it. He expected her to say something, but she shook her head instead and turned back to pictures on the floor. "I hate it, but I get it. So we have to find something else."

Later, when Jaime had made no move to stop him from spending another night and they were lying in bed, sated, but still not tired enough for sleep, Sean couldn't help turning toward Jaime and asking, "Can I see the other pictures? The ones you don't want to turn in?"

"It's cheating to ask me that right now," Jaime said as he traced his fingers down Sean's bare chest.

"I prefer to think of it less as cheating and more as asking you things when you're in a really good mood."

"Cheating."

"I'm just curious. You never actually said why you don't want to turn them in."

"I'll show you if you promise me one thing," Jaime said as he sat up. "You have to promise not to argue with me about it."

"That means I'm going to want to."

"I know. And that's why I didn't tell you about them. Aleksandra's annoyed. She wants me to be able to turn them in because it was Anastasia's idea, and Anastasia wants to tell her story. But she never should have picked me to help her do it. Aleksandra does understand why I won't turn it in. She doesn't like it, but she gets it. I'm not sure you'll get it."

"Explain it to me, and I can try." Sean figured he should not point out how many times Alana had thrown up her hands and declared that there were some things she just couldn't make him understand, no matter how many times she tried.

"No arguing," Jaime said again, as he got up and opened the drawer to his desk to pull out a portfolio just like the one he'd used for the pictures he'd decided to turn in a few hours ago.

"I won't argue." Sean sat up, pulling the blankets over his lap as he did.

"Okay." Jaime sat back down next to him, but instead of handing over the portfolio the way Aleksandra had, he kept it as he opened the first page to show Sean. It was a bright shot taken outside in the sun. Anastasia was looking up at the camera from where she was seated on the grass. Her blonde hair was shining from the sun behind her, and it looked like Jaime had caught her laughing. "Anastasia's a dance student here. She also knows Aleksandra from this bikini bar where they used to work. But Anastasia also strips."

Jaime turned the page to a very different picture of Anastasia on a pole. It was clear she was nude, but the angle Jaime had taken it at cast shadows in just the right places.

"She's not ashamed of it or anything. It pays for school. She also does sex work, and while she agrees it's not healthy for everyone, maybe not even her, she thinks there's too much shame in it. She knows other girls who do it, and they don't just hide it from their families. They hide it from their best friends and their roommates. She runs her own ads and picks her own people. She says she's not going to do it forever, but she's fine with doing it so she won't have to take out loans. Most of the time. Sometimes she admits she hates it, but she's not willing to give up the money yet. She gave Aleksandra the idea to do a series for *her* project, and agreed to let her into the hotel rooms after her meetings. Of course, Aleksandra told her I should do it instead. Aleksandra is amazing at movement. Every shot she got of you dancing is clear in a way I couldn't manage, but that's not really what they wanted for this."

"These are really good. I mean, I know it's not really my thing, but I think these are good," Sean said as Jaime flipped through the next few pictures. Most of them were in hotel rooms. Sometimes she was on the bed, but there were also a few of her standing by the window. There was one of Anastasia taking off her makeup in the bathroom and one of her smoking a cigarette outside on the sidewalk. There was something so different in her eyes compared to the first picture that Sean felt like something was breaking inside him when he reached the end.

"I know," Jaime whispered as he closed the portfolio and set it on the bedside table.

"And she wants you to turn them in."

"Yeah, and I feel kind of like a jerk that I can't do it after she let me in. I should give them to her and let her do whatever she wants with them without crediting me, but I haven't been able to do it yet."

"So why can't you use them?"

"Some of the best collections are going online. If I turn these in, they could end up online with my name attached to them. I can't chance that." Jaime looked at him like that should make sense.

"Why?"

"My family would see it. I can't have someone search me online and have these show up on the school website. We're Catholic. My mom goes to Mass three times a week. She'd go every day if she didn't have to work so much. When I go home next week and I have to go to confession, I'm going to have to start with how I lie to her every week about going to mass, and then move on to the sex and finish with how I hang out with sex workers, and even then, it won't feel right because I'm not going to stop doing any of those things. The priest can't tell her any of that, but if these show up online, she's not going to think it's amazing. She's just going to be angry and ashamed of me."

"You're not giving her much of a chance to surprise you," Sean said.

"You promised not to argue." Jaime leveled him with a look, but Sean had a built-up resistance to the same kind of looks from Travis.

"I'm not arguing. I'm observing. Didn't Jesus hang out with prostitutes?" Sean asked, and got a glare as an answer. "It was just a question, but I'm done."

"I just can't. Aleksandra gets it. Her parents still think we're engaged because that helped them get over her living with a guy. She just has more leeway because they're in Russia. She only brought it up because she wanted me to tell you about it."

"I'm glad you told me," Sean said, lying back down and pulling Jaime with him. "I don't get it completely. My mom would think it's amazing, but I'm trying to get it."

"I know. She'll like my theme for my graduate exposition anyway. Of course, Lupe was helping me with it, but now that's not going to work. Do you think Alana would help? I can probably change some things so I can use more than one subject."

"Probably. She likes you. What did you want to do?"

"I'm still figuring it out." Jaime reached behind him to turn off the lamp. "I need to do that before I try explaining it to anyone else."

Sean wasn't sure Jaime could see his nod, but either way, Jaime draped his arm over Sean's waist and kissed the back of his neck the way he always did when he was tired and just wanted to sleep, so Sean let it go.

"TRAVIS GAVE her a good evaluation. He was always going to, unless she stopped coming to classes, but she didn't ask about auditioning for the company again. I guess she'd asked a few weeks ago, and he told her to audition for the summer program and then finish school, since she only has a year left. He thinks she's reconsidering auditioning at all now." Sean hadn't expected Jaime to ask. Lupe had been a forbidden topic for the past two weeks, and he'd given up trying to get Jaime to talk about anything that was going on with her.

"Yeah. She mentioned that before. I think she feels like Alana's ahead of her because she's about the same age, and then she found out you auditioned out right of high school. I was hoping Travis would tell her to finish college, since he has a degree." Jaime turned on his side in the bed so they were facing each other, but it was too dim to read his face.

"Does it bother you that I didn't go?" It had never bothered Sean before. A lot of dancers didn't end up at college, and it had made sense to start his career earlier. He could always go to college when he retired, if he wanted. But Jaime wanted Lupe to finish, and he was finishing a master's degree himself.

"No. I wouldn't have minded if she'd had a chance earlier and skipped college. It's just that she's almost finished now. She might as well finish with a year and a half left." Jaime paused and sighed the way Sean was learning meant he trying to make himself say something he didn't want to say. "When she found out and we fought, part of why she was angry is she thinks she can't audition now. She's wanted this for years, and she was hoping to get a scholarship for the summer program and then audition after she graduated. Now she thinks she can't unless she pretends she's fine with us dating, and she's not. She said I could have dated anyone, and I picked the one person that fucked up her life."

"That's still her problem. She's the one making it hurt her career," Sean said. When Jaime didn't answer, his mind started drifting to all the things Jaime had already done to help Lupe with her career. He'd helped her with money; he'd made Aleksandra drive her to the last week of classes, even when they weren't speaking.

"Are you going to break up with me for her?" he blurted out as his heart started to pound from the thought.

"No." Jaime reached toward him and ran his fingers through Sean's hair. "No, babe, that's not what I'm thinking. Sorry if it sounded like that."

"Did you think about it?" Sean didn't want to know the answer, but when Jaime didn't respond as quickly, that told him enough. "You did."

"I thought of a lot of things. A lot of those things were really stupid, and that's why I didn't want to talk to you right away. I didn't want to say anything I'd regret, and I would've regretted that." Jaime moved his hand from Sean's hair to cup his cheek. "I know this might get worse. It's probably going to get worse, so I did think about it. But I decided I wanted to be with you. That's what matters, right?"

"Yeah."

"I'm sorry I thought about it," Jaime added.

"It's okay. You're right. You couldn't not think about it— especially if she told you to." Sean shifted closer and pushed Jaime onto his back so he could curl against Jaime's side. He could relax when Jaime's arms immediately moved to hold him. "She can still audition, no matter what happens. Travis is fair, and if he decides not to be, Steph makes the final decisions. She's only going to take her talent and dedication into account. Travis and I auditioned together, and she took us both. Then she made us dance together even though Travis hated me and thought I was a spoiled brat. Amy competes with Alana, and nothing Steph and Travis do is ever going to make them get along. So aside from being really awkward, there's no reason she can't still join the company no matter what happens."

"And the summer program?"

"She can still get in."

"And get the scholarship? She can't do it without the scholarship, and she said she'd never get it now," Jaime said.

"There's more than one. Some of them are partial," Sean said, although he knew where this was going to end up.

"You're not telling me something," Jaime said after a minute. "Is this what you feel like when I don't tell you what's going on?"

"There's only one scholarship that pays all the tuition and helps with housing expenses during the program. I usually just let Travis pick it. He's better at that stuff, and if I pick, he ends up arguing if he doesn't like who I pick, and the one time that happened, there ended up being two that year."

"So you have a say in it?" Jaime asked.

"My family sponsors it. It was my idea to start it. We give money to the arts anyway, and I wanted Travis to stop bitching about how not everyone got to go to an arts boarding school and whatever summer programs they could get into," Sean said. "And you're going to be a way better person than you should be and ask me to let her have a fair chance no matter what happens, aren't you?"

"You don't want to?"

"I don't know. Right now I'm still hoping she'll realize she's overreacting, and by the time she has to audition in March, it won't matter. If she makes things worse for you, I'd rather sit through all the video auditions with Travis and try to convince him someone else is better. Sorry. I can't pretend it doesn't matter if she hurts you while you're still doing everything you can to help her. She should realize how amazing that makes you, and if she doesn't, I kind of want to fuck her over. I guess I'm not as good of a person as you are. I was supposed to sit in on her evaluation, and I only sat in on Michael's instead. Don't worry. It didn't hurt her grade. It just made me look unprofessional."

When Jaime didn't answer right away, Sean started to wonder if he should apologize. The problem was he didn't really want to apologize.

"Thanks," Jaime said instead.

"What are you thanking me for?" It was better than the defense of Lupe he'd expected, but it made even less sense.

"I don't know. Being pissed off for me when I'm the one who lied about being with you? You don't have to be. I was kind of an ass about it."

"Have you talked to her about us since it happened?" Sean asked. He could feel Jaime's muscles tense under him at the question.

"Not really."

"But you're still on the same flight home tomorrow," Sean said.

"It's going to be a long flight."

"Do you think she's going to tell everyone when you get to Arizona?"

Sean wasn't surprised when Jaime seemed to ignore the question. It was the most he'd gotten out of Jaime about the subject in the past two weeks, and it was only a matter of time before Jaime closed off and said it wasn't worth talking about.

"No. I met you because of her. She's afraid they'll blame her for that. We'll pretend things are fine, and come back from Christmas and ignore each other again."

"Maybe it'll get better. Maybe if she sees you're still the same over Christmas when she has to see you, she'll get over it. She was fine with me and Michael before."

"No." Jaime's voice was tight, but he didn't cut Sean off like he had when Sean had tried to make the same point before. "She was fine with you because she sees it as your own choice. She thinks it's wrong, but she forgives it like she forgives everything else that's a sin, like lying and cheating. But she wants me to admit it's something wrong when it's not. Maybe that would work if she just put all sex outside of marriage together, but she's not. She doesn't want me to stop having sex until I get married. She wants me to stop being gay or admit it's something I should try to stop doing. She can't forgive me if I have no intention of changing what's wrong with me."

"She can't forgive you because there's nothing wrong with you."

"That's debatable," Jaime whispered back as if he didn't want Sean to hear.

"It's not." Sean backed away enough that he could prop himself up on his elbow and look down at Jaime. When Jaime looked away, he slid his hand over Jaime's cheek and urged Jaime to meet his eyes. "There's nothing wrong with you. I admit that I don't really think much about God, and I don't go to church. But Alana does, and she says you can't think being gay is wrong if God made you that way, because he wouldn't make you gay if he didn't want you to be gay. So there's nothing wrong with you."

"Sean." Jaime whispered his name. His eyes had gotten glassy as Sean spoke, so when he closed them and turned away, Sean let him.

"If I can't convince you, I'm going to have to ask Alana to help because she knows more about it." Sean settled down back on Jaime's chest and let his fingers trace patterns over Jaime's skin.

"That sounds like a threat," Jaime said after a minute.

"It's not. I just want you to believe it. There's nothing wrong with you—except that you think putting dandruff shampoo on your face to get rid dry skin makes more sense than using moisturizer. That's wrong. You have to stop doing that."

"It worked." Jaime laughed as he leaned down to kiss Sean. He sucked on Sean's bottom lip for a second before biting lightly and backing away.

"Because it probably chemically dissolved your skin or something. I'm texting you every day you're gone and reminding you that you promised to stop doing that."

"Okay," Jaime said, but he must not have missed the hint Sean was moving toward because he squeezed Sean a bit tighter against him before adding, "I'll text as much as I can, and I'll let you know when I can get away to call, but it might not be a lot. I haven't seen my mom or my brothers in a year, so they're going to want me around."

"That's okay. I see my mom every few months, and she's still going to act like it's been that long." Sean hesitated before adding, "Just let me know you're okay every once in a while so I worry less."

"You don't have to worry about me."

"Yes, I do, and I'm still in New York for another week, so I can bother Aleksandra if you just tell me you're fine all the time."

CHAPTER 16

SEAN TRIED to let his family distract him through Christmas. It worked most of the time because Jaime kept his word and kept up a steady stream of texts. Jaime had to share a room with his younger brother at night, so Sean could excuse the lack of good night phone calls. He couldn't blame Jaime for not wanting to share that with a sixteen-year-old, and Jaime always sounded fine during the short phone calls when he'd managed to sneak away.

Sean was sitting on the couch ignoring the smirks Elizabeth was giving him while he texted Jaime. The kids were already in bed, and she didn't really mind him ignoring the conversation she was having with their mom so he could text Jaime instead.

Sorry. I have to go. Lupe decided she wants to talk. I will text you later. I know you're already worrying, but stop.

Sean tried not to react, but he must have done something, because when he looked up, they had both stopped talking and were watching him instead. Sean looked back down at his phone and opened a window to text Travis instead.

My mom is worse than you.

He saw Elizabeth get up and leave the room, but he kept his eyes on his phone in hopes that they'd think he was still texting Jaime and give him space.

In what context? Travis sent back.

Nothing important. Good Christmas?

Sean should have known Travis would text back, *What's wrong?* instead of answering his question.

Lupe has ignored Jaime all week. Now she wants to talk to him.

Right. Stop freaking out. Maybe it's good. If you don't know yet, it's too early to freak out. Calm down.

Sean sighed. It was exactly what he'd texted Travis to hear, but it didn't help.

"Honey?" his mom said next to him, and he had to look up.

"Yeah?" Sean looked back down long enough to text Travis that he'd failed at calming Sean down fast enough that his mom wouldn't notice something was wrong.

"Is everything okay with Jaime? You haven't been talking to him that much during the break. You haven't even been talking about him."

"He's busy with his family. He doesn't get to go home a lot, so it makes sense. But I just miss him. That's all," Sean said.

She didn't answer right away, and that was first clue he wasn't going to get away with the answer. If she'd bought it, she would have hugged him and reminded him that they'd be back together in New York in a few days.

"Do they know about you?" she asked.

"His cousin does," Sean answered. He knew she'd hear in his voice that Lupe knowing wasn't a good thing.

"Lupe, right?" she asked, and Sean nodded. "How does she feel about it?"

Sean sighed and shook his head. There was only so much he could do to pretend that he was fine, and he couldn't do it when he had to sit around waiting to find out if Jaime was okay with whatever Lupe wanted to talk about.

"She hates me. She hates that he's gay, and he keeps saying he's fine, but I know he's terrified she's going to tell his whole family." Sean looked away from her and leaned forward to hide his face in his hands instead. She didn't answer him right away, but she moved closer and rubbed his back the way she had when he was eight and he'd come home from school and asked her why they'd never told him liking boys wasn't normal.

"He's twenty-four, and he hasn't told them in all this time?" she finally asked.

"They're not like you guys." As Sean said it, he couldn't help remembering when he'd pressed Jaime about it the first time. At the time, his simple "Your people change, not my people" had sounded ridiculous. That was before Sean had seen it.

"What is he going to tell them if you stay together? Or is he just planning to break up with you before he has to?" she asked. He wanted to be surprised that she didn't just comfort him the way he wanted her to, but he wasn't. If he hadn't known somewhere in the back of his mind that she wouldn't, he would have called her right after Thanksgiving.

"That's not really what I'm worried about right now." He wanted to feel better from the comforting arm around him, but he couldn't.

"Maybe you should be," she said. "If he's not ready to tell his family, he doesn't have to, but that's not healthy for you."

Sean sat up and turned to look at her. He tried to see it from her point of view. She didn't know Jaime. She was worried about her son, who seemed unhappy. A few months ago, Travis had almost told him the same thing. But that wasn't enough because it was one thing for Travis to tell him he shouldn't get involved in the first place. Pushing Jaime away after already committing to him was a different story.

"You think I should leave him just because it's gotten hard? He told her he was staying with me no matter what she said. It's not his fault his family isn't like mine."

"I'm not saying it is. But it's not your fault either. It's not fair for him to put you through the stress of hiding a relationship when you don't have to. That's not your problem, and he's hurting you by making you deal with it."

"It's my problem because I care about him. Yes, the situation sucks and it hurts, but *he's* not hurting me. He didn't put himself in a bad situation so I'd have to go through it with him. I knew he wasn't out to them before we even started dating. He told me." Sean stood and turned away from her. "I decided I wanted to be with him then and I'm not blaming him now because I care enough to hurt when he hurts. I can't believe you are."

"He shouldn't ask you to deal with it."

"He didn't ask me. He never asked me to. I just said that I would because I care." The most ridiculous part of this whole argument was that Jaime still wasn't asking him to do anything. He was still saying he was fine. He was still telling Sean not to worry.

"Sean, you can't change people. Sometimes they just aren't right for you," she said from behind him. Her voice was calm like it had always been. She had never yelled when he was growing up, like she knew it would make it impossible to yell in return even if he wanted to.

"I can't do this with you. I'm tired and you're not helping. I'm going home tomorrow—to New York," Sean said before walking to his room. She called after him, but she didn't follow or knock on his door when he closed it behind him and started to pack. Jaime still hadn't texted him back when he'd finished and bought a new plane ticket for the next afternoon flight, so he texted Travis again instead. Maybe she meant well, but he couldn't worry about Jaime and argue with her about it at the same time. At least he could count on Travis to know his limits.

I'm going home tomorrow.

Go ahead and buy me a plane ticket. I'm not letting you sit in the apartment with Alana for five days without me. It will be a mess when I get back.

Thanks. I'll e-mail it to you.

He was already in bed and trying to fall asleep when his phone buzzed with a text from Jaime.

It's ok for now. Annoying, but nothing bad. Stop worrying. Sorry I can't call right now, but I'll try tomorrow.

Sean typed out an *okay* and his thumb hovered over the letter L for a second before he changed course to letting Jaime know when he'd be on the plane with his phone off instead.

ELIZABETH DIDN'T ask questions when he asked her to take him to BART the next morning, but she passed the station and drove him all the way to the airport instead. They were almost there when she turned down the radio.

"Mom told me what happened last night," she said.

"Do you agree with her?"

"I don't know." Elizabeth glanced at him for a second before turning back to the road. "I'm worried. I know he hasn't said he loves you, or you would have told her that last night, but you wouldn't go through all this and fighting with Mom over it if you didn't love him."

"I haven't told him either," Sean said.

"That's fair," Elizabeth said with a short nod. "And that doesn't make her right either. They found out Eric had student loans and bad credit, and they thought he was marrying me for the money. They said he was going to bring me down, and I should wait to marry him until he'd paid everything off. Then when I didn't want to do that, they said I should get a prenup. They're all about not conforming to gender roles, but they don't like that he stays home with the kids."

"Why didn't you ever tell me that?" Sean tried to think back to when she'd started dating Eric. He'd already been out of high school, so it wasn't like he'd been too young to understand any of it.

"I wanted you to like him, and I wasn't sure you'd get it. Why didn't you tell me about Jaime's family?" Elizabeth turned to look at him as she pulled into the airport.

"I wanted you to like him, and I wasn't sure you'd get it."

"I'll give him a chance," Elizabeth said. "Let me know when you're home safe."

CHAPTER 17

"DID TRAVIS call you, or have you just been living in our apartment the whole time we were gone?" Sean said when he walked in the apartment to find Alana on the couch watching TV.

"You'd cry if your plants died without Travis to water them, but yeah, he called me." Alana moved over on the couch so he could lay down with his head on her lap. "Have you heard from Jaime?"

"Not really. I got a text he must have sent while my phone was off, and I let him know I was here, but no answer. He's probably busy." He closed his eyes as she ran her fingers through his hair.

"Yeah. Did you sleep at all last night or on the plane?"

"I couldn't." Sean felt himself start to relax as she massaged his scalp. "I haven't heard his voice in three days, and he says he's fine, but he always says he's fine. He'd say he was fine if he were in the hospital with a brain injury. I can't be sure unless I can hear him and see him."

"I know. But he'll be back in four days. He booked his flight in time to be home for New Year's Eve just for you. So you'll know then."

"I think I love him."

"We figured," Alana said as she picked up the remote to mute the TV. "It's okay. Go to sleep. I'll wake you up if he texts or calls. I told Travis to text my phone when he gets in so you wouldn't get your hopes up for nothing."

When Sean woke up hours later, the TV was still muted, and there was a pillow under his head instead of Alana.

"I know," Travis said in a hushed voice behind him. "But that's all we can do. We can just be here."

"I can't believe you're not flying to Arizona to yell at him or something," Alana said.

"I think he's trying. I don't think there's anything I can do that would actually make it better, and he hasn't actually gone a day without any communication."

"Until now."

Sean sat up, and they both turned to look at him. Travis had the decency to look at least a little guilty for talking about him.

"The day's not over yet," Travis said. "If you're up, I'm making dinner and you're eating it."

"Thanks," Sean said as he stretched and got up to sit next to Alana at the kitchen counter. "Not just for the food. And technically, he texted me this morning while I was on the plane."

Travis nodded and glared at Alana when it looked like she was going to give an opinion. When she rolled her eyes and got up to take the TV off mute, Sean was pretty sure she put it on Lifetime just to spite them, but it helped that the movie she found made so little sense that Travis picked on the stupidity of it for the entire hour until Sean's phone finally vibrated.

I'm sorry. I can't talk tonight. I just can't. I don't know if I can talk tomorrow either.

Are you ok?

Sean could feel Alana and Travis watching him as he stared at his phone, hoping for at least one answer. They weren't even trying to pretend they were doing anything else. After a minute of nothing, Alana reached over to squeeze his knee.

I'm fine. Stop worrying.

It was the shortest of the long variety of *I'm fine* messages he'd gotten in the last two weeks.

"You don't actually think that means he's fine, do you?" Alana said. Travis had the decency to not look over his shoulder to read, but it wasn't like he had to when Alana was there to do it for him.

"He's usually more specific. He's fine, but all his cousins are over, and he can't get any time alone, but he'll promise to make an excuse to go to the store tomorrow and call me then."

"But you at least got a lot of texts from him yesterday, so it hasn't been that long," Travis said.

"That was before Lupe decided she actually wanted to talk to him," Alana said before he could say it himself.

"You're not helping. If you're not helping, you're going home," Travis said over his head when Sean ran his hands over his face and then kept them there to block them out. When he didn't move, Travis's hand settled on the back of his neck. "You should get some more sleep. You're still tired."

"I slept half the day."

"So you didn't sleep last night if you're still tired." When Sean didn't move, Travis added, "If something's wrong, you can't do anything now, and if you don't make yourself rest, you're not going to be able to help if he wants your help later."

"Why are you being so nice to him?" Sean's words were muffled behind his hands, but Travis could understand him when he was drunk and brushing his teeth, so he didn't expect any different now.

"It's less about being nice to him and more about keeping you from going crazy." Travis squeezed his hand for a second before standing up and pulling on Sean's arm until he stood up after him. He pushed Sean toward his bedroom that he hadn't even bothered to enter. "Get in bed. I'll let Alana come in and sleep with you after she promises to sleep and not make you freak out some more."

Sean stopped when they got to his door.

"What?" Travis asked when he resisted Travis's attempts to push him inside and held on to Travis's arm instead. "I'm not tucking you in. This is as far as I go. You can undress yourself or sleep in your jeans. That's up to you, but I'm not sure how you even slept on the couch in jeans that tight."

Sean's laugh didn't sound happy, even to his own ears.

"I know. It's just—" Sean shrugged. "Thanks for trying and giving him a chance and flying all the way back here before you were supposed to. You didn't have to."

"You're welcome," Travis answered before pushing him inside. "Now get some sleep."

SEAN HEARD nothing all of the next afternoon, and the text he sent to Jaime went unanswered. When the day moved into evening, he gave in and texted Aleksandra to see if she could at least confirm that Jaime was busy, but that went unanswered also. It was dark again when his phone rang with Aleksandra's ring tone.

"Please don't tell me he's fine. I know he's not fine. Please just tell me what's wrong," Sean said, leaving out a greeting the way Jaime always did.

"I know. I'm not. And he's really sorry he can't call you himself. He hasn't even been able to call me. It's taken him all day just to get a few minutes of privacy every few hours to tell me what happened in a million texts, and he could have done the same with you, but he thought it would be faster and easier if I called you because texts aren't personal anyway. Please don't be mad he texted me first. I think it's just that it's easier to keep himself together for me."

"It's okay. Just tell me what happened."

"You knew Lupe wanted to talk to him. She wanted him talk to someone at their church about not being gay or something. She said she wasn't going to tell anyone, but she wanted him to get help. He wasn't happy about it, and I don't think he was going to do it, but it wasn't that big of a deal," Aleksandra said. "But I guess his older brother overhead some of the conversation. He didn't figure it out, but Enrique asked him about it yesterday. He thought Jaime was having problems with me or cheating on me, and Jaime just kind of brushed him off, so he went to Lupe."

"She told him?" Sean asked.

"She did, and he told everyone. He expected them to just kick him out, but they didn't. Personally, I wish they had. Instead, his mom canceled his flight back to New York. She's demanding that he speak to someone in the church about some kind of counseling. He has his phone, but she won't let him use her car, and they live in the middle of nowhere. He can't get more than a few minutes alone to text. He can't even call me because there's always someone listening. She's making him sleep in the living room because she doesn't want him sharing a room with his little brother. It's really fucked up."

"I can buy him a plane ticket. Just tell me what day." Sean reached for his laptop on the coffee table. "He'll need a ride to the airport, right? If you give me the address, I can figure something out. There has to be a car service."

"Sean, it's not that simple," Aleksandra said instead.

"I know." Sean sighed. "But I can't do anything else, and I don't think he'd want me to fly there. So I can fly him back tomorrow. I don't care how much it costs. Unless he wants me to fly there. I can fly there."

"Wow. Okay, I appreciate the response that you'll do anything. I do," Aleksandra said. "But it's not just that. If he leaves, they're never going to let him come back."

"He wants to stay?" Sean's chest physically hurt as he said it.

"Sean, I don't think he knows what to do. It's only been a couple days, and he's upset, but you need to let him decide to come back on his own." Aleksandra paused, but Sean could tell she had more to say. "Look, if you beg him to come back, he might, but then you'll always be the guy who made him leave his family. I can't make you listen to me, but I really think if you just let him know you're there for him while he figures things out, it'll be better."

"Can I text him? Does he want to talk to me, at least?" Sean wasn't sure what he'd do if she said no.

"You can. He does want to talk to you. He just kind of has to sneak around to text without them looking over his shoulder, and he can't really talk without someone listening, so he thought it would be easier if I called than if you had to find out with sporadic texts over two days like I did. He's still Jaime, and he's trying to protect you even when you don't want him to. He's not used to letting people take care of him, even me, but that doesn't mean you can't try."

"I'll try."

"If you want to stay up late, that's your best chance to text him. That's what I did last night. Eventually his family will go to sleep, so tell him to text you when they do, and he'll stay up. His mom is a light sleeper, so he can't talk—or that's what he says. I think they've just got him so paranoid at this point that it's not worth it fighting with him about it. It's like they're breaking him down by never leaving him alone and making him sleep in the living room. So now he just doesn't want them to try to take his phone when they figure out he's texting. He pays for it, so they can't, really, but it's easier on him if he doesn't have to fight about anything else. But he'll text you after they go to sleep if you want."

"Thanks."

"Thanks for not just giving up on him. Call me if you need to. I have to go to work tonight, but I'm keeping my phone close in case things get worse and he needs me."

Sean stared at his phone after she hung up. When Travis and Alana didn't ask questions right away, he realized how quiet they'd been during the whole call.

"You heard all that, didn't you?"

"You keep your phone volume really high," Alana said.

"I'm stupid," Sean said when neither of them added anything.

"What?" Travis asked.

"I'm stupid. You were right when you met me and you said I was stupid and spoiled and I didn't know anything about the real world. I haven't gotten any better. I told him everything would be fine, and now I ruined his life, and I didn't even think about it."

"Sean, no," Travis said. "I'm not going to argue that maybe you should have thought about some of the consequences before, but that's pointless. Either way, you didn't make him gay, and that's their problem, not you. They don't even know you. This was probably going to happen eventually, because with you or not, he's still gay."

"I don't know how to help him. I don't know how to take care of people. I flew you all the way back here because I couldn't handle this. I can't do that for him, and I don't know what else to do."

"You'll figure it out. As much as I hate to remind you, you're pretty much the only person who took care of me when I got injured and had surgery. You take care of people just fine when you have to. This is just a different thing to figure out."

"And he's probably easier than Travis," Alana added. "He's probably not going to barricade himself in his room with twenty cans of ravioli and refuse to shower for eight days."

"There were painkillers involved in that event," Travis said before she could add anything else. "The point is that you can handle this. Just let him know you're here when he needs you, and you'll help him however he wants you to help him. Aleksandra's right. You need to let him decide on his own to come back. Just make sure he knows you'll be here when he does."

"That doesn't feel like doing anything," Sean said.

"I know," Travis said. "Look, I haven't done a damn thing, and you paid to fly me back here anyway. Does it help just that I'm here?"

Sean nodded and looked back down at his phone.

"Then just knowing you're there for him will help, even if you can't physically be there."

Sean opened his text conversation with Jaime.

I talked to Aleksandra. I'll stay up as late as you need me to if you want to text me. I'm here for whatever you need.

It was an hour before he got a single text back that Jaime would text him again when he could, and then nothing for hours. Alana eventually went to sleep in his bed after Travis argued that one of them should sleep. A little after two, his phone finally vibrated.

Sorry. I know it's even later in New York. Enrique stayed late and I couldn't get him to go home. And I'm sorry I couldn't tell you everything myself. I just couldn't.

It's okay. I understand why. Don't worry about me. Can I do anything?

Sean could feel Travis watching him from where he was washing out the coffee pot. He'd made Sean drink tea instead, claiming he couldn't handle Sean being any more jittery than he already was.

Thanks. There's not really anything anyone can do. Lupe actually texted to say she's sorry. She didn't think he'd tell everyone. Her mom won't let her talk to me now. My mom says she's a bad influence and her mom says I am.

Sean was still trying to figure out how to answer him when another text came through.

She was supposed to fly back with me tomorrow, but I'm not sure if her mom is letting her go back. Does Travis know anyone at Purchase who can find out? Lexi doesn't want to stalk her dorm and I don't know any of her friends.

"He wants to know if you can find out if Lupe is back in New York tomorrow," Sean said. "I don't know why he cares. I really want to tell him to stop caring what happens to her."

"If you thought that was the right thing to do, you wouldn't be saying that to me instead of him. I have Michael's number. They're in the same dorm, so he can probably find out. I'll call him tomorrow."

Travis says he can probably find out from Michael tomorrow.

Thanks. I just don't want them to make her drop out and transfer somewhere here because of me.

"You shouldn't tell me what dorm she's in if I ask," Sean said aloud as he typed back.

It's not your fault. You didn't do anything to her.

If it wasn't for me, my mom wouldn't be fighting with her sister. Lupe wouldn't be worried she'll never join Steph's company. And I think you probably flew home because you fought with your family about me. You didn't have to. I'm sorry.

Sean started to type a response, but nothing felt like enough. Instead, he caught Travis's eye and nodded toward Travis's room.

"I'll be awake if you need something. If you don't, let me know so I can go to sleep," Travis said before leaving to give him some privacy.

Aleksandra said you couldn't talk, but you called her and she talked to you. Can you do that? I'll talk and then we can hang up and you can text me back. You don't have to if you don't want to.

It was only a few seconds before his phone rang.

"Hey. If you want to say something, you can just hang up and text me whenever you want, and then if you want to call me back after I read it, we can do that too. It's okay that you can't talk, but I wish I could hear your voice, so I figured maybe you'd want to hear mine.

"Please don't worry about me and my mom. It's nothing. I promise. I know her. She'll probably call me tomorrow and we'll talk about it, and it'll be fine. She didn't like it when I turned down San Francisco Ballet and moved to New York, and she didn't like it when I moved in with Travis, and she's gotten over all that. So really, don't worry about me at all. I'm fine. Travis is here. Alana is trying to move into my room. So just let me worry about you. I know I don't really get what you're going through, but I'm trying.

"I just want you to know I'm here. If you want to text me. If you want to call me and listen to me talk."

Sean could hear Jaime breathing on the other end of the line when he paused. He knew what he needed to say next, but there was still part of him that had to fight with himself to say it. As much as he knew Aleksandra was right, he could admit to himself that he'd still rather beg Jaime to come back to him.

"And I want you to know that as much as I want you to come back, you can take whatever time you need, and I'll be here. If you want to come back, we can figure that out, but I'll be here until then."

He could hear Jaime breathing for a few seconds, and then there was a beep in his ear from Jaime hitting a key. When Sean pulled the phone away, he saw that Jaime had hung up. He felt like he couldn't breathe evenly as he waited to see if Jaime had hung up so he could text something.

Thank you. For everything you said. It did help to hear your voice. I had a hard time making myself hang up so I could tell you that.

Call me whenever you want, Sean answered.

Sean knew it might be pathetic that he was willing to sit by the phone like that, but he could make an exception for the circumstances.

I'm sorry I can't come back yet. I know I promised you I'd make New Year's Eve.

Sean could admit to himself that his heart clenched, and a part of him that he wasn't proud of wanted to demand Jaime come back like he promised.

It's okay. The girl Travis was trying to date definitely dropped him, so it's better if I hang out with him. I miss you, but it's okay.

It was a full minute before Jaime answered. Sean was starting to worry someone had heard him.

I miss you too. I should sleep and you should get some sleep. I'll text when I can.

Sean agreed, even if he didn't want to. It was late, and Jaime probably couldn't sleep late if they were making him sleep in the living room, and now that he'd gotten off the phone, he could feel how exhausted he was. He stumbled to Travis's door and leaned against it.

"I'm going to sleep," he called through the door.

He heard movement and stood up in time not to fall over when the door opened.

"You okay?" Travis asked.

"Not really," Sean admitted. "I told him I'd do whatever he wanted and I'd give him as much time as he needed, and I think maybe it helped."

"Do you not mean it?"

"I do. I want to do whatever helps him," Sean said. "But I also really just want him to come home. I want to hear his voice so I can figure out how he's really feeling, because he still didn't really tell me. I know why I can't, but I still just want to put him on a plane and bring him home because I'm selfish, and I want him here."

He wasn't surprised when Travis stepped forward and pulled him into a hug. He'd let the tears he'd been holding in slip out because he was too tired to care anymore. Despite Alana's jokes about them, they'd never really had a physical friendship, but when he cried, it was like Travis didn't know what else to do. So he'd hold Sean and it helped, except this time what Sean really wanted was to have Jaime's arms around him instead. They stood still for a few seconds until Sean managed to take a deep breath and pull away.

"Thanks." Sean wiped his hand over his face. "I'm just going to brush my teeth and crash."

Travis nodded and let him walk away. When he got out of the bathroom a few minutes later, Travis was back in his room, but his door was still open and Sean waved away his concerned look as he passed by. Alana was fast asleep, but the weight next to him was enough of a comfort that he could let his exhaustion pull him into sleep.

CHAPTER 18

SEAN WOKE to an empty bed. There was enough light in the window that it was obvious Travis had decided to let him sleep in. He picked his phone up before he even bothered to sit up, but there was only an e-mail from Elizabeth asking how he was doing. He'd have to remember to e-mail her back after he felt like he could function.

Travis and Alana turned to look at him when he came out of his room. Alana was sitting on the couch with her laptop—probably because Travis had overruled her and turned the TV to the History Channel.

"Hungry?" Travis asked.

"I want a shower first, but yeah."

"I got a text from Michael. He hasn't talked to her, but Lupe's back in the dorm. His roommate saw her."

"Thanks." Sean sent a text to Jaime to tell him, but he wasn't surprised when he didn't get an answer back.

When he walked back out of the shower, Travis's door was closed, and Alana had turned off the TV. He didn't think anything about it until he'd come back out of his room dressed and Alana was too quiet.

"What's going on?" He looked at Travis's door and then back at her.

"I don't really know. He took his phone in there ten minutes ago," Alana said. "I tried to listen at the door, but he's too quiet."

"You don't know who he's talking to?"

"Okay. I do. Well, I'm not sure, but I think it's Michael," Alana said.

"Do you know why?"

"Not really. When he told Travis that Lupe was home, he wanted to know why Travis was asking, and Travis didn't tell him. Then a few minutes ago he started texting Travis. I guess when Travis didn't tell him anything, he decided to confront Lupe."

"And?" Sean asked when she didn't continue.

"And I don't know. Travis stopped telling me what the texts said and locked me out of his room."

"You can pick that lock."

"He knows that. I think he used a chair."

Sean knocked on Travis's door harder than he probably had to.

"If something's going on, I should get to know about it," he called through the door.

When Travis opened the door a few seconds later, he was off the phone.

"I'm not really sure you want to know this," Travis said.

"Why?" Sean let him pass, but he followed Travis to kitchen.

"Because if I tell you, you're kind of obligated to tell Jaime. He would want to know, and you're probably not going to want to tell him. *I* don't want you to tell him." Travis pulled eggs out of the refrigerator and turned on the stove as he spoke. "I'm not his boyfriend. If I want to withhold information for his own good, I can damn well do whatever I want, and I think you should let me."

Sean thought for a minute before asking, "Can you tell me why you don't want him to know? Is it possible to tell me without telling me what it is?"

Travis focused on the omelet he was making instead of answering, and Sean let him. Travis would talk when he was ready. While he waited, Sean played on his phone and read over every text message he'd gotten from Jaime since Thanksgiving to remind himself Jaime cared about him. Jaime would come back. And when he came back, it wasn't going to be just so he could break up with Sean like his family wanted him to. Eventually, Travis put the omelet on a plate in front of him and came around the counter to sit on the stool next to him.

"She wants to tell him something, and she got Michael to trust her enough to pass the message to me. I told him he couldn't call you himself and he's scared enough of me that he listened, and Lupe's not going to do it herself either. I don't trust her. I know you don't trust her."

"But Jaime will want to," Sean filled in.

"His judgment with her doesn't seem to be that great," Travis said.

"I don't want to know. I really don't want to know, but if he knows I know there's a message and I kept that from him…."

"So tell him that, and then tell him I'm not telling you. Because I'm not."

"Travis."

"I'm not talking about it. The end. I'm not telling you what she said, and I'm not telling him. I'm also not telling Aleksandra after he gets pissed off and sends her after me. You can all just be pissed off at me if you want, because I don't give a shit."

"I'll let that go until I talk to him," Sean said. He knew exactly how that would go. If he wanted to ignore it and eat his omelet, it wasn't like Jaime had been able to answer his last text anyway.

"I'm not changing my mind either way," Travis said before getting up and going into the bathroom without looking back. A minute later, the shower started, and Sean had no choice but to give up for the moment.

His phone vibrated, but it was only Aleksandra.

I don't know what you said, but he seems a little better. It's possible he's lying to me because he's only texting, but he doesn't usually. Sorry I demanded some of his limited texting time, but I'm sure he'll text you later.

He'd be lying if he said part of him wasn't jealous, but if things were reversed, he had to admit he'd text Travis as much as Jaime, so he texted back to thank her for the update and settled on the couch with

Alana. Half an hour later, when he got a new text, he almost didn't want it.

Did Michael say anything about Lupe besides that she was back? Did he talk to her?

"You can just tell him the truth," Alana said after he showed her. "Travis still isn't going to talk."

He did and he called Travis about it, but Travis won't tell me what he said.

Why?

He doesn't think it's a good idea to tell you and if he tells me, I'll tell you.

Jaime answered faster than Sean expected, but maybe he didn't have time to think about his answers if he didn't have much time in general.

Did you actually ask him or are you letting him not tell you because you trust him?

I do trust him, but will ask him again anyway for you. He probably won't tell me. He's really stubborn when he thinks he's right.

"Travis!" Sean yelled toward Travis's door without getting up. He'd only come out of the shower a few minutes before, so Sean wasn't surprised when he came out of his room shirtless.

"Why are you yelling? There's not a fire." Travis threw on his tank top as he walked to the couch and sat down.

"What did Michael say?"

"No," Travis said without even pausing. He picked up the remote and started scrolling through the screen guide.

That's not fair. Travis barely even knows me.

Jaime's next text came before Sean could answer.

Do you know if Lupe wants me to know whatever it is?

Sean groaned, and part of him wished he hadn't pushed Travis at all so he wouldn't even know that much.

"Want me to steal your phone and tell him I did it?" Alana asked.

"No." It would be easier, but he wasn't about to cut off what contact he had by choice.

She does. But I asked him again and he said no.

Ask him seriously.

Sean sighed, but he took the remote from Travis's hand.

"Okay. You have to tell me. He knows I don't really want you to, but he's right. He has a right to know. So what is it?"

"No."

"Travis."

"I'll tell you that she's fine. She's not injured. She's not dropping out of school. She's not starving. There's no reason to worry about her. That's all I'm saying."

I asked him. I promise. And I got confirmation that she's ok. She's not dropping out of school. And that's it.

When Jaime didn't answer, Sean tried sending an apology.

"Travis. He doesn't believe me and he's mad at me. That doesn't help things."

An hour and no texts later, Travis must have realized Sean was starting to edge toward mad.

"If it makes you feel better, I'll call Michael and tell him that I'll go there tomorrow and talk to her in person. She can try to convince me that she deserves to talk to him then," Travis said.

"She made Michael call you when she could have called on his phone. She's too scared to talk to you herself."

"She showed up to a week of classes and her evaluation when I was mad at her. If she cares about talking to him as much as she cares about her grades, she'll talk to me."

"Okay. Call now. Call him right now."

"No listening at the door," Travis said as he got up.

"If that worked, Alana would have already told me what was going on."

The twenty minutes Travis was in his room made Sean wish Alana hadn't given in when her mom asked her to come home. He fiddled with his phone and reread every text message Jaime had sent him in the last few days. He opened the computer and made himself answer Elizabeth's e-mail. He was sure his response ended up rambling and panicky. He jumped in his seat at the sound as Travis's door opened, and Travis didn't even mock him.

"She agreed to meet me on campus tomorrow afternoon. I'm not making any promises, but I'll talk to her. If I think it's a good idea for Jaime to hear anything she has to say, I'll let her e-mail me whatever she wants through Michael, and you can send it to Jaime."

"She could send it from his e-mail directly to me."

"And then you'd have to send it, even if she sent something stupid." Travis sat back down next to him on the couch. "Trust me. Let me handle this. You worry about Jaime and yourself."

Sean gave up and nodded as picked up his phone to tell Jaime about the meeting. He copied Aleksandra on it to save Jaime the time later. At least he knew Jaime would answer that if he could, so Sean could relax a bit during the hours he had to wait before he got a response.

I wasn't mad at you. I know you're trying. I knew if you were letting Travis not tell you, it was because you want to help me. But thanks for getting him to go talk to Lupe. I want to talk to her, even if you all think it's a bad idea.

It was late enough that the lack of sleep made Sean get up from the couch so he could lie down and text Jaime from his bed, but still early enough in Arizona that Sean doubted he'd have a long time to talk.

How are you doing? Sean asked instead of giving in to the urge to beg Jaime to come home.

The same. I e-mailed the school that I had a family emergency and might have to take a semester off. I'm not sure I'll be gone that long, but I don't want to just not show up if it gets worse.

Is there anything I can do?

Not right now. I have to go, I told my mom I'd go to mass with her. Get some sleep. I think they suspect I'm texting at night and I want to talk to you, but they won't let me sleep late, so I'm exhausted. I'll sleep tonight and stay up tomorrow for you, ok?

Sean swallowed his disappointment and texted back an agreement. The last thing Jaime needed was to exhaust himself.

TRAVIS WAS already gone when Sean stumbled into the living room the next morning, but Alana was back.

"He just left," Alana said. "He said to tell you that he's not meeting with her until four, and then they have to actually talk, so try not to send him a hundred texts asking how it's going. He left early because he wanted to go pick up some things from the studio before he went. But then he contradicted himself and said to text him if you started to freak out or something happened or if I thought maybe something might happen, so you can probably just ignore that and text him as much as you want."

Sean settled on the couch next to her and tried to listen to her commentary on the movie. He ate when she told him to eat and went through stretches and a minor workout when she pointed out they'd been too lazy since they'd come back. As the day stretched on with no word from Jaime, he caved a few times and let himself text Travis so Travis could tell him to stop worrying.

When Aleksandra called at four thirty, he was still in the shower so he wouldn't cave and interrupt Travis, but Alana called through the door that she was on the phone.

He rinsed his hair and dried off just enough that he wasn't completely dripping when he wrapped a towel around his waist and stepped out to take the phone.

"Have you heard from him at all today?" Aleksandra asked.

"No. Have you?" Sean answered.

"Sorry. He's probably just busy. I just haven't heard anything, and I was worried. I was hoping he wasn't answering me because he only had time to text you or something. But that's stupid. He can text fast enough to tell me that in between texting you."

"I've been telling myself he hasn't had time," Sean admitted. "Do you think something's wrong?"

"No. Sorry. I told Alana not to make you get out of the shower, but she said you'd want her to. I'm just worried and I haven't heard from him either. He'd be mad I called and made you worry more for no reason."

"It's okay. I get it. I'm worried too."

"I also wanted to know if you'd heard from Travis how things are going with Lupe. I got impatient."

"He hasn't called. He promised he would call as soon as he could. So they're still talking."

"So I'll let you get dressed. Just call me if you hear something, okay?"

Sean handed the phone back to Alana after he hung up. He didn't bother repeating his instructions to get him if anything happened in the few minutes it would take him to get dressed.

"He's probably okay. Maybe he hasn't been able to charge his phone or something. He's kind of hoping they forget he has it, so maybe that's all it is."

Sean was saved from arguing with her when Travis called.

"Hey. We're not having a long conversation about this because I have to get home and you can argue with me there," Travis said.

"You still don't trust her."

"She didn't bother trying to lie to my face, but I don't think it'll do any good for him to hear what she has to say. That's it. You can tell Aleksandra that, and if you want to argue about it, we can do it when I get home."

"But it's going to be like arguing with a wall, isn't it?"

"Well, you can tell Jaime you tried."

Jaime didn't answer the text he sent, and Aleksandra just sent back a text that Travis was probably right anyway.

When the day turned into night without any message from Jaime, Sean decided he didn't have the energy to fight with Travis if Jaime hadn't asked him to. He sent a text to Aleksandra at eleven and she confirmed that she hadn't heard anything either, so he turned all the alerts on his phone to the loudest settings and followed Alana to bed. If he slept through everything, she'd wake him up.

But when he woke up, Alana was sitting next to him on the bed with her laptop open.

"He didn't send anything. Aleksandra didn't either. You have an e-mail from your sister, but the subject line didn't imply Jaime randomly contacted her, so I let you sleep," Alana said before he even asked. "I wasn't sure if I should take your phone in the living room so I'd hear it, or if you'd panic if you woke up and it wasn't here."

"Thanks."

"Travis said he's opening the studio for us because if you sit by the phone again all day, you'll go insane, but he's going to let you leave your phone on the whole time."

"I can't just go in and dance."

"You can always just go in and dance. You might as well take advantage of your best friend having keys so you can go in during vacation. It'll help."

It was only the knowledge that arguing with Travis was more exhausting than listening to him that made Sean go out in the cold when he didn't want to. He demanded they take a cab instead of the train, and Travis just let him pay for it instead of lecturing him on how stupid it was to waste the money. He sent a text to Aleksandra on the way, asking her to text him if she heard anything, and ended up promising the same thing to her.

Travis let them warm up without pushing, and hooked up his iPod to the speakers so he could find the piece he'd started choreographing before the break. He tried to work them through his ideas for only half an hour before he declared they were too distracting and he remembered why he always worked alone until he was finished and taught them the steps later.

When Travis decided it was a better use of their time to work on areas in which they needed improvement, Alana glared at Sean's unresponsive phone harder than he did, but she didn't argue. His head wasn't as focused as it could have been, but Travis switched to having them go through some of his favorite older dances so time moved faster than it had during the last two days of sitting on the couch by the phone. By the time Travis agreed they deserved dinner, Sean was at least worn out enough that he might be able to sleep.

Jaime still hadn't sent a single text after dinner and Alana offered to stay the night, but he was pretty sure she was running out of clothes in Travis's closet, and while he appreciated the comfort, he could stand to have some privacy for the night. He was trying to decide how late he should stay up when he got a text from Aleksandra.

Can I come over tomorrow? I can't sit alone in this apartment another day and not hear anything.

Sure. Come over whenever you want.

He texted his address and gave her Travis's number in case he somehow slept through his phone ringing before giving up and trying to sleep.

CHAPTER 19

HIS LIMBS still felt heavy when he gave up trying to sleep the next morning. His subconscious couldn't stop worrying that he'd miss a text or a phone call, and he'd found himself waking up every two hours to check. Travis didn't bother asking if he'd heard anything when he wandered into the living room and lay down on the couch with the blanket from his bed.

"Why did you even get up if you're sleeping on the couch?" Travis asked when he didn't move or even turn on the TV for thirty minutes.

"I was bored." Sean pulled the blanket tighter around him before Travis could get any ideas about taking it away.

"You're still not doing anything." Travis came to stand behind the couch and leaned over him.

"Fine," Sean mumbled. "I was lonely. The bed was too big. I kept waking up and hoping he would be there."

"Are you going to stay on the couch until Aleksandra gets here? She's already on her way. If you're still like this, she's going to tell him how pathetic you were." Travis tugged at the blanket, but when Sean held on, he gave up easily.

"It won't matter if I never see him again."

Travis moved around to the front of the couch and kneeled in front of him.

"You can't think like that."

"I haven't heard anything in two days. What if he decided he didn't want to come back? What if they shipped him off to one of those stupid treatment centers where they try to make people not gay anymore? The last thing he said was he was going to mass. What if they didn't let him leave?"

"He's twenty-four. I don't think they can force him to really do anything," Travis said as he picked up his phone to read off the screen. "I'm going to go let Aleksandra in. She'd probably appreciate if you at least got dressed."

Sean let Travis pull him up so he could get dressed and make it into the bathroom before Aleksandra saw him. He felt a little more awake after he'd washed his face, but he was sure the dark circles under his eyes wouldn't go away, no matter how expensive his eye cream was.

Aleksandra was seated at the counter with a cup of coffee, but she got up when he came out of the bathroom and came over to wrap her arms around his waist. He held her and let his head drop to her shoulder.

"If he doesn't have a good reason for not calling, I'm going to kill him. I'm going to throw all his stuff out the window and not let you help him bring it back into the apartment." Aleksandra took a deep breath before she pulled away. "I hope you didn't think I was coming to cheer you up. I came here so I could be with someone who will worry as much as me."

"That works for me," Sean said as they sat back down at the counter.

"Also, I'm tired of eating pasta, and clearly someone is feeding you."

Sean expected some kind of a complaint from Travis, but he opened the refrigerator without even rolling his eyes.

"Do you want breakfast or lunch?" Travis asked.

"Are pancakes an option?" Aleksandra asked.

Aleksandra pulled her phone out of her purse and set it on the counter next to Sean's while Travis started mixing the pancake batter.

"When you said you would fly him home or fly there to get him, were you serious?" Aleksandra asked after a few more sips of coffee.

"Yeah. Do you think I should just go?" Sean was already remembering the flight times he'd looked up yesterday before she answered.

"Not yet, but if he doesn't call, would you fly me there in a few days? I know you'd probably rather go, but I might have better luck. I've met his mom before at least once."

"Yeah. I'll fly you tonight if you want and fly you both back tomorrow if you can get him to come, or I could just go with you to Arizona and not go to his house." She might not be able to bring Jaime back right away, but at least she could tell him what was going on. He wouldn't just be sitting at home waiting for some kind of news.

"Sean, that's—" Aleksandra started, and then paused like she had to rethink her words. "Okay, I don't care if Jaime said I wasn't supposed to ask you this. If he doesn't want me to ask you, he should have called me. Do you realize how expensive it would be? Did you win the lottery at some point, or does Steph pay a lot more than Lupe thinks? Because Jaime would never notice you wear three-hundred-dollar jeans, but you just offered to fly both of us back to New York on New Year's Eve."

Sean couldn't help hesitating and looking at Travis for help.

"If you don't want people to notice, you could buy Levi's," Travis said, but Sean could hear the tension in his voice.

"Sorry. You don't have to answer that," Aleksandra said. "I know I shouldn't have asked. I just didn't want to take you up on that and then find out you cleaned out all your savings. Jaime would really never forgive himself."

"I didn't win the lottery. It's a trust fund from my grandparents. I don't actually buy a lot of expensive clothes, and I still get paid by the company, so I'm not blowing through it or anything. I know how much it is, but it's not a big deal." Sean sighed. "I would have told him eventually."

"For what it's worth, he's not dating you for it. He had no idea until I asked, and even then, it's not like they couldn't have been a gift. Mostly I had to explain to him how jeans could even cost that much. There may have been a comment about how maybe they had some kind of security measures because they were hard to get off."

Sean laughed, and he couldn't help pushing the button to light up the picture of Jaime on his phone.

"I just want him back." Sean ran his finger over Jaime's face on the screen. "If you think you can go there and get him back, it's worth it."

"If he doesn't call tonight, I'll go tomorrow. I don't think you should go to his parents' house. He wouldn't want you to have to deal with them if you don't have to, but if you want to fly with me and hope I can bring him to you, I'm not going to stop you."

Sean nodded as Travis set pancakes in front of them.

"I know he was planning to come back. He didn't want to get your hopes up about how soon it would be, but he told me that. It meant a lot to him that you said you'd be here when he got back. Last time I talked to him, he said you were the only thing helping him keep it together. That's why I'm worried. If he's not calling you, then it's because he *can't.*"

"We could just go to the airport right now," Sean said.

"Sorry," Aleksandra said as she put her hand on his shoulder to stop him from getting up. "That was supposed to reassure you, not upset you. I think we should give him one more day. I told you I wasn't going to be cheering you up, but I should have mentioned I'm also bad at comfort."

"But what if he's not okay?" Sean couldn't help letting his mind travel back to the idea they'd locked him up somewhere, no matter how much Travis told him they couldn't.

"I'm sure he's okay. Maybe they stole his phone or something and he hasn't gotten a new one, but I'm sure he's fine," Aleksandra said. "I promise. If I didn't think so, I would have called you this morning and begged you to fly me there."

"But you'll go tomorrow?"

"I will, and you can go with me if you want," Aleksandra said. "I know he just wants to give them a chance. He thought they'd kick him out and when they didn't, he decided he owed them something. He doesn't like giving up on people, but sometimes you have to."

Sean nodded, but he didn't bother trying to pretend anyone he'd given up could compare to Jaime giving up his family.

Travis ignored them most of the day. He refused to let Alana come over because he said there was only so much he could handle, but Sean noted that he still hung around the apartment. He never disappeared into his room for more than an hour at a time, and he made them food before Sean even realized he was getting hungry.

"I can see why Jaime's so worried about Travis hating him," Aleksandra said when Travis left to take a shower.

"Travis never hated him. He just thought I shouldn't be dating him," Sean said.

"Still, he's a good guy. If he was a jerk and he hated Jaime, it would matter less."

"When Jaime comes back," Sean said, because he had to think it was *when* and not *if*, "I'm going to make Travis tell him that he doesn't hate him."

"I'm not sure he'll believe it if you make him do it," Aleksandra said. "But I have a feeling Jaime will figure it out."

When Sean's phone lit up and started blasting Jaime's ringtone, Sean jumped for it.

"Jaime?" Sean held Aleksandra's hand as he strained to hear through the sound of running water.

"Sean? I'm sorry. Can you even hear me?" Jaime's voice was muffled, but it was there.

"Yeah. Are you okay?"

"I'm sorry. I'm running the shower and hoping they don't hear me. I'm stupid. I've been sleeping with my phone, but I didn't think about sleeping on top of the charger or something. My mom says I must have just lost it, but I know I didn't. I'm sorry. I just got all your texts and a million from Lexi."

"It's okay. We were worried but it's okay if you're okay," Sean said, although he wanted to point out how obvious it was that Jaime was anything but okay. "Did you get a new one?"

"No, but Victor, my little brother, passed me his when no one was looking. Fuck, he is my favorite brother. I'm apologizing for every time I let Enrique pick on him. Enrique can go fuck himself." Jaime's words were muffled, so it was possible Sean was imagining the cracks in his voice.

"You're not okay," Sean said instead of asking.

"I'm sorry. I've been trying. I'm okay sometimes. I know you're already worried enough. I'm mad, but I'm okay," Jaime said.

"Please don't tell me you're okay if you aren't. I'm supposed to worry about you. Also, I have Travis, and Alana, and Aleksandra here if I need anything. If talking to me about how not okay you are helps, I'd rather you do that."

Jaime was quiet, and Sean couldn't even hear his breath over the sound of the shower for a minute.

"I don't think I can do this anymore," Jaime said, just as Sean was starting to worry he'd said the wrong thing.

"Do you want to come home?" Sean didn't realize he'd said "home" instead of New York until after he'd said it.

"Yeah. I just have to figure it out. I can maybe take a bus or something if you can look up tickets for me. I don't even know how. Maybe Aleksandra can do it, and I can pay her back," Jaime said.

"Let me fly you. I'll buy you the ticket tonight and order a car for you tomorrow. I can text you the information if you can check it. Does Aleksandra have the address where you are?"

"Sean, that's expensive. I can't just let you pay for that."

"Yes, you can. You can let me. I know it's a lot, but I want to. I can afford it, and I want to do it. Please just let me get you home." Sean knew he was close to begging, but if Jaime was ready to leave, he didn't want to wait more days to see him.

"I can't ask you to do that for me."

"I'm not, okay?" Sean could only hope the same logic he used on Travis and Alana would work on Jaime. "I'm doing it for me. I miss you, and I want you home. I want to hold you and fall asleep with you and wake up in bed with you. And if you want to come home, I want to do all those things tomorrow instead of five days from now. So I'm asking you to do it for me."

"Babe, that's bullshit," Jaime said, but Sean could hear the smile in his tone.

"Fine. If you want to believe I'm selfless, when both Travis and Alana will tell you I'm a spoiled brat with no patience who is used to getting what he wants, we can go with that, but I still want to do it."

Sean waited a few seconds before adding, "And Aleksandra agrees you should let me buy the plane ticket. She's been worried. She said something about throwing all your stuff out the window, so you might want to come back."

"Okay," Jaime said, "Yeah, okay. I guess if you want to do it."

"I do. I really do. I'll book everything right now." Sean looked at Aleksandra and shared a relieved smile.

"Sorry. I have to go. I had to charge my phone some before I called you, and I should look like I actually showered, but okay. Lexi has all my information and you can text me when to be ready tomorrow."

"Thanks. I'm not lying about the selfish thing. It just happens to work out for you, but I'll see you tomorrow."

"Tomorrow," Jaime whispered before he mumbled a good night.

"Sorry," Sean said to Aleksandra after he hung up. "I meant to let you talk to him, but he didn't have a lot of time."

"It's okay. I can yell at him tomorrow." Aleksandra smiled and hugged him.

"What are you going to do when he realizes you really are a spoiled brat?" Travis said from behind him.

CHAPTER 20

JFK WAS so packed with people flying into New York for the holiday that Sean didn't even have room to pace the floor near security. The plane wasn't late, but he'd dragged Aleksandra to the airport two hours early because, even in the morning, the city was getting impossible to travel around. So of course that meant Jaime's plane was delayed an hour. Aleksandra was just as restless as he was, and every time he sat down and tried to be patient, she just took a turn getting up and trying to pace around. Maybe he should have taken Travis up on his casual offer to come with them, but he didn't think Jaime would want extra people if he was still upset. He'd only sent a few texts in the morning, and they only confirmed he was on the plane. There was nothing about how it had gone when he'd left the house.

Sean's phone vibrated, and he stood as he took it out of his pocket. It was nothing more than a simple *I'm here*. Aleksandra didn't bother to ask what it said. It was enough that Sean stood and focused on the doors letting people out of the secure area.

It was only a few minutes, but they seemed to drag even more than the three hours he'd already waited. When he finally saw Jaime walking toward him, Sean couldn't help weaving through the people between them to meet him halfway. Jaime smiled when their eyes met, but it was weak, and Sean could see the pain and exhaustion under it. Sean had always thought airport reunions were romantic. He'd never had one, but he'd always pictured starting one with an intense kiss while he was oblivious to everyone but the guy in front of him. Instead, he ended up pulling Jaime into a hug, and holding on seemed more important than pulling back far enough for a kiss. He ended up with one arm around Jaime's waist and one around his shoulders so he could cradle the back of Jaime's head where Jaime pressed his face into Sean's neck. Sean blinked back the tears because he was supposed to be the one giving comfort. Jaime was taking deep breaths, but it felt more like he was trying to breathe Sean in than like he was holding back sobs. Jaime left a soft kiss on his neck, but he made no move to pull back for more.

"*Te amo.*" It was whispered below his ear, but Sean caught it and gasped before he could stop himself and pretend he didn't understand. Jaime let out a short chuckle at his reaction.

"Those would be the two words you know besides *loco*," Jaime said.

"I might have looked it up on purpose," Sean said, and he pulled back just enough that he could see Jaime's reaction as he answered. "I love you too."

Jaime leaned down for a kiss, and Sean opened to him, letting Jaime's lips move over his until Aleksandra spoke a while later.

"This is all very romantic and adorable, but I missed you too."

Sean had to force himself to let go when Jaime pulled away from him to hug her, but they broke apart soon enough, and Jaime reached for him and threaded their fingers together right away.

"Do you want to get on the train to our place, or go back to Sean's because it's closer?" Aleksandra asked.

"Our place. I just want to crash in my own space, even if it takes forever to get there." Jaime squeezed Sean's hand and looked over at him. "Is that okay?"

"Whatever you want is okay," Sean answered.

"I'm asking because I'm assuming you're coming with me," Jaime said.

"Do you honestly think I'm going to say I need to go home because I have better things to do after I admitted that I love you, and I haven't seen you in three weeks?" Sean tugged his hand to move them toward the train, and when Jaime laughed, it sounded a bit less hollow than the last one.

The train grew less crowded as they left the city, but it still seemed too public to try to talk about anything. Jaime sat next to him, and he didn't resist when Sean took his hand. Instead, he slouched in his seat so he could lean his head on Sean's shoulder. In a few minutes, his grip on Sean's hand relaxed, and he was breathing evenly. Aleksandra gave them a smile before pulling out her headphones. Sean couldn't sleep, and he hadn't thought to bring any kind of entertainment, so he had an excuse for staying still and watching Jaime sleep. He closed his eyes after a while, but found himself listening to the sound of Jaime's breathing instead of drifting off.

He opened his eyes as they neared White Plains. It was awkward to reach around and stroke Jaime's cheek without jolting him, but it was worth the strain on his shoulder when Jaime's eyes fluttered open after a few soft words, and he leaned into Sean's touch.

"Hey. We're here," Sean whispered.

Jaime rubbed his eyes as he sat up, and he still seemed groggy as Sean led him out of the train and pulled him into a cab. He only seemed to wake up after Aleksandra opened the door and led them into the apartment.

"I thought it would be more like home if I left it a mess. Also, you didn't contact me for three days, so you can live with the dishes," Aleksandra said. "I had to go to Sean's and get Travis to feed me."

"I don't even care right now. I can do them later," Jaime said, and pulled Sean after him as he walked past her to his room.

"Are you really going to go have sex without telling me what happened?" Aleksandra called after them.

"No. Just let me change, and you can come in. I just want to lie down."

Jaime slipped out of his jeans and boots before digging through a drawer to pull out pajama pants Sean had never seen. He looked toward the open door before walking toward Sean and pulling him close again. He held on like Sean was the only thing holding him together, so Sean squeezed him just as tight and didn't let go until Jaime's arms relaxed. He stepped back only a few inches and left his head down on Sean's shoulder as he took several deep breaths.

"It's okay. I'm here. I'm probably not leaving until you kick me out," Sean said as he let his hands stroke down Jaime's back.

"I'm not kicking you out."

"Well, then it's until Aleksandra kicks me out or Travis decides to drag me out. It could go either way."

Jaime chuckled and lifted his head off Sean's shoulder to give him a quick kiss before calling out to Aleksandra that she could come in. He pulled back his sheets, and Sean didn't hesitate in slipping off his shoes and climbing in after him or moving under Jaime's arm so he could rest his head on Jaime's chest. Aleksandra settled on top of the blankets on Jaime's other side.

"I left while my mom was sleeping," Jaime said. "The car was early, and I packed after I got off the phone with you. I woke up Victor and told him I was leaving, but I didn't wake her up. I should have, but I didn't want her to argue with me. So I just left without saying anything." Jaime glanced at his phone where he'd left it on the bedside table. "She hasn't called, and my phone's already dying again."

"We can share my charger until you get a new one," Aleksandra said.

"Thanks." Jaime looked back up at the ceiling. "She probably won't call. I need to believe that, anyway. If she does, I can deal with it, but I can't wait for it. Victor might eventually, but not now. She'll be paying too much attention, and he can't risk it. They didn't even want me talking to him. She actually moved me into the living room because he's a minor, and she thought I was going to molest him or something. Enrique actually told her he was sorry he couldn't take me to his house for her, but he had to think of his daughter's safety. She's six months old. I can't even be a bad influence, so it's obvious what they think will happen."

"They're wrong," Aleksandra said while Sean was still trying to process everything. "You know they're wrong."

"I know," Jaime said. "I'm contacting Lupe tomorrow. I'll go through Michael because they'll watch her phone records, but I'm contacting her. If she's the only member of my family who wants to talk to me, I'm going to do it."

"And you want to do it tomorrow?" Sean asked.

"I need to know what she wants. She sent one text after they found out, and it wasn't bad. She just said she was sorry, and she wouldn't have told Enrique if she thought he'd act like this. If she wants to stay in contact, I want to. If she doesn't, I'd rather find out and get it all over with." Jaime paused to look down at Sean. "I know you don't want me to, but I don't need Travis to protect me. I can't even fathom how he's decided that's his job."

"You don't know him well. He never hated you, and even if he did, it wouldn't matter. He really did hate me when we first met, and when I needed a place to crash after I broke up with my ex, he let me move in." Sean was already gearing up for Jaime's argument over the implication that he was a damsel in distress, but Jaime stayed silent longer than he expected. "He has a hero complex or something. If you don't want his advice, that's fine, but if it made him overprotective, whatever she wants to say can't be good."

"You can stay if you want. If she really wants to talk to me, she can talk with you there," Jaime said. "I won't kick you out for her again. If she can't be nice to you, I'll make her leave."

"Are you sure?" Sean couldn't help asking. He wasn't about to ask Jaime to push away the only family he seemed to have left.

"I'm sure."

"I'm just assuming that I'm staying," Aleksandra said. "If you try to kick me out, I'm calling Travis and inviting him to this party."

"I was going to let you stay anyway. You can leave out the threats," Jaime said. "But I'm kicking you out now. I want to sleep."

Aleksandra grumbled about how it was only nine o'clock, but she got up and flicked off the light as she left.

"Sorry," Jaime said after she'd closed the door behind her. "You're probably not tired, but I slept three hours last night."

"It's okay. I didn't sleep much either."

Sean moved away so he could peel off the jeans he'd left on before. By the time he'd tossed them out of the bed, Jaime had taken off his shirt and tossed it aside also. Jaime turned on his side facing him, and their eyes met in the dim light as Jaime ran his hand down Sean's back and let his fingers slip under the hem of Sean's shirt.

"I thought we were sleeping," Sean said as Jaime pushed his shirt up to feel skin.

"We are. I just want to feel you with me."

Sean sat up enough for Jaime to get his shirt off. He barely breathed as fingers skimmed over his chest and down his arms.

"I was afraid I'd never see you again," Sean whispered as Jaime cupped his cheek.

"I know. I'm sorry."

"It's okay. You're here." Sean's lips brushed against Jaime's as he spoke, just before giving in to a soft kiss. Jaime pulled back to look at him, and Sean was just about to lean in to continue the kiss when Jaime turned to face away from him. Before Sean could worry, Jaime reached back and pulled Sean's arm around him. He backed up until his back was flush with Sean's chest, and relaxed when Sean kissed the back of his neck.

Sean could almost believe Jaime had fallen asleep. His breathing was even, but his hand still had Sean's in a vice grip where he'd pulled it up to his chest. After a few minutes, Jaime sucked in a harsh breath and his chest tensed under Sean's hand.

"Jaime?" Sean whispered against his neck, but Jaime shook his head.

"I'm fine," Jaime whispered back. "Go to sleep."

Sean wanted to point out that he couldn't be fine. He wanted to do more than pretend he didn't hear the small sniff in front of him, but instead he pressed himself closer against Jaime's back and held him tighter.

"I love you," Sean whispered in the dark.

Jaime didn't answer, but he brought their joined hands to his lips to kiss the palm of Sean's hand. It didn't feel like enough, but if all he could do was hold Jaime until it was over, he'd do it.

SEAN PUSHED around the food on his plate more than he ate breakfast. He'd texted Travis back that, yes, he would be back in classes on Monday because the company didn't stop for him, but he hadn't mentioned Lupe was coming over. He'd wanted to. If it was inevitable, he wanted to know everything Lupe had to say in advance, but he didn't have to ask to know that Jaime wouldn't want to involve Travis anymore.

"You don't have to stay," Jaime said from across the table. "If you're worried about seeing her, you don't have to be here."

"I'm worried," Sean admitted. "But I'm not leaving as long as you want me here. I can handle it."

Jaime didn't look convinced, but he nodded anyway.

When Lupe knocked on the door a few minutes later, Sean took a deep breath and hung back with Aleksandra while Jaime answered the door. He wasn't sure what to expect, but it wasn't for Lupe to launch herself into Jaime's arms.

"I'm sorry. I'm so sorry, and I'm sorry I couldn't see you in Arizona. I tried, but they all made it impossible, and it seemed like I might have more luck if I came back here. I tried to get Michael to text you that I wanted to talk to you, but he told Travis, who decided that was too vague of a message to give you," Lupe said before she even released him.

"That's all the message was?" Jaime glanced back at Sean as he pulled back from the hug.

"It's all I wanted to say through other people," Lupe said. "I guess you know he came over here and he didn't like my answers to his questions."

"Sort of," Jaime said as he led the way farther into the apartment. Lupe hesitated as Jaime sat next to Sean, but then she seemed to steel herself before she took the chair across from them. Sean stopped midway to resting his hand on Jaime's back, and forced himself not to glare at her for making him feel like he had to hold back at all.

Lupe said something in Spanish, but Jaime shook his head and interrupted.

"Don't do that. Don't speak Spanish so he can't understand you. I told you he was going to be here. You're not going to be rude to him."

"Fine," Lupe said in English this time. "Look, I love you, and I know you're a good person. I know all that stupid stuff my mom said about you being dangerous was wrong. I know you'd never be some kind of awful child molester. If Enrique had given me any hint that he was going to say any of that shit, I would never have told him anything."

"Thanks," Jaime said. Sean didn't think it deserved thanks. Not thinking someone was a child molester for no reason wasn't actually an amazing compliment. He clenched his hand to keep from pointing this out, only because he'd promised to let Jaime talk to her without starting any arguments.

"If you don't want to get help, I won't keep pushing you. I can love you like I love Michael, and I can forgive you just like I can forgive any other sin. It's a little harder because you're more than just my friend, and you can't confess and ask forgiveness if you don't intend to even try to stop, but I can do it."

Sean held his tongue as he waited for Jaime to tell her off.

"Okay," Jaime said instead.

"What?" Sean couldn't help blurting out.

"Sean." Jaime said it like a warning, but that just made it more impossible to hold his tongue.

"That's not okay. You're not doing anything wrong. There's nothing to forgive you for in the first place. That's bullshit," Sean said.

"I'm trying to be tolerant of your beliefs," Lupe snapped before Jaime answered him. "You could try to be tolerant of mine."

"Why should I tolerate the idea that something is wrong with who I am? It's not like I'm lying or hurting anyone. I'd be lying if I tried to be something else. It's offensive to say something is wrong with me."

"Sean, please." Jaime rested his hand on Sean's arm.

"Do you agree with her?" Sean asked. Jaime hesitated and looked between him and Lupe before looking down at the floor instead of either of them.

Sean felt his chest tighten as the urge to kick Lupe out of the apartment grew. Instead, he tried to pretend she wasn't sitting there and watching as he reached for Jaime's cheek and coaxed Jaime to look at him.

"Just tell me the truth. Be honest. I'm not going anywhere," Sean said.

"Maybe. I don't know," Jaime said.

Sean nodded even though the words broke his heart. This wasn't a conversation he wanted to have in front of Lupe, and he had a feeling a single conversation wasn't going be enough, anyway.

"It's not true. There's nothing wrong with you or us, but I'll just have to work on showing you that."

Jaime nodded, but Sean was sure it was to acknowledge his words instead of a sign of agreement. Sean followed Jaime's gaze back to Lupe, who was looking at her phone instead of them.

"I have to go," Lupe said when she looked up again. Her eyes flicked to Sean, but she only focused on Jaime. "I borrowed my friend's car and she needs it back, but I'll e-mail you and we can have lunch on campus sometime next week, okay?"

Sean watched as they said good-bye and hugged again at the door. After the door closed behind her, Aleksandra broke the silence.

"Just so you know, I agree with Sean. Actually, I agree with Travis," she said. "That was not good for you. All that bullshit is worse than Enrique. If she makes it look like she's being nice, it's going to make you believe that stuff."

"She's trying," Jaime said.

"No, she's messing with your head and acting like she's showing growth by tolerating what she thinks is wrong with you," Sean said. "That's fucked up."

Sean stood and walked to him. He took both of Jaime's hands in his and leaned into him to touch their foreheads together.

"You're amazing, and you're strong. You take care of everyone around you even when they don't deserve it. There's nothing wrong with you. If you want to believe in sin, then it would be a lie to try to be something you aren't."

"You don't think I should see her either, do you?" Jaime asked instead of agreeing with him.

"I don't."

"She's the only family I have now. I can't lose that."

Sean didn't argue, even though he wanted to point out that Aleksandra was worth more than Lupe. Instead he nodded and asked, "Do you want me to drop it for now?"

"You're not just going to drop it altogether, are you?" Jaime asked.

"You just admitted you might agree there's something wrong with being gay. I think at some point we should talk about that," Sean said.

"I'm sorry," Jaime mumbled, his gaze dropping from Sean's face to the floor.

"I'm not mad. I'm worried."

Jaime groaned, and Sean thought he was going to pull away, but he buried his face in Sean's neck as he shook his head.

"I think I could handle it better if you were mad."

"Maybe," Sean admitted. "But I'm not actually trying to make you feel bad here."

"I'm not seeing a shrink," Jaime said. "Don't get any ideas about dragging me to one."

"Right now I'm just thinking that you've made me want to hide you from Alana twice in two days. I'm not telling you why, because you're not going to like that one either." Sean pulled Jaime toward the bedroom and tried to ignore the voice in his head telling him he'd never actually succeeded in getting Travis to talk to anyone after his surgery. This was different, and Travis had ended up fine. If he concentrated on how Alana was going to mock him forever if she ever knew he'd ended up comparing Jaime to Travis in his head, he could deal with the rest of it later.

For the moment, Sean settled for pushing Jaime onto the bed and lying down on top of him. Jaime's hands settled on his hips as Sean rested his head on Jaime's shoulder.

"Can you at least tell me she can't convince you to try to be straight?" Sean asked.

"I've tried that already—before anyone knew I wasn't. Long before I even met you. I already know that won't work. I'm not trying again." Jaime's hand drifted up his back, his fingers grazing along

Sean's spine before stopping at the base of his neck and tugging lightly on his hair.

"Okay. So I have plenty of time to figure out how to make you okay with that."

"I am okay with it," Jaime said.

"You're okay with it, but you also think it's kind of wrong? That doesn't make any sense."

"It's complicated, but I'm fine with it." Jaime rolled them over so he was lying on top of Sean. He trailed his lips down Sean's neck, biting down just enough that Sean groaned and couldn't help pushing up against him.

"I know what you're doing. I know you're distracting me so you don't have to talk about this," Sean said.

"You said we didn't have to talk about it right now." Jaime pushed his hand under Sean's shirt as he talked. "It's been three weeks. I'd be doing this if you wanted to talk about anything on the fucking planet."

"Which is why it's going to work," Sean said against Jaime's lips before giving into a kiss that let him forget everything else.

TRAVIS WAS in his room when Sean came home Sunday evening, but he was cooking when Sean came out of the shower. He set a plate on the counter for Sean without asking and let him take a few bites before he spoke.

"Michael told me you saw Lupe. I figured you would. If you would have told me, I would have told you what she was going to say so you were prepared."

Sean pushed around his food instead of answering, and Travis gave him time to think about it.

"Jaime didn't really want me to," Sean admitted after buying himself time with a few more bites of food. "You're not really his friend, and all this stuff with his family is kind of private. You can get that, right? You're the same way. You didn't even want Alana to visit you for a week after your surgery. I know it's not the same thing, but it feels like the same idea."

"I think I remember you telling me that wasn't healthy," Travis said.

"It wasn't. But he's got me, and he's got Aleksandra, and we both agree with you about Lupe as it is. I get why you got involved. I asked you to find out if she was back, and that made Michael call you about it, but Jaime wants you to stay out of it." Sean expected Travis to argue, but he nodded instead, so Sean took his chance with something he was even less sure would go over well. "And I told him he could come over here without worrying about dealing with you. He's not happy with you. You knew that was going to happen, and I want him to come over this week, so if he wants to ignore you, you'll just have to get over it. He's not going to fight with you, but you can't expect him to keep trying to win you over."

"That's fine, but I'm still saying something if he's an ass to anyone besides me," Travis said.

"He wouldn't do that. He just wants you to mind your own business—which I personally gave up on a long time ago, but he hasn't realized you're incapable."

"I'm capable. Just not with you, because you can't function without help."

"I can function just fine."

"You still don't know how to do laundry."

"I know how to hire a laundry service."

CHAPTER 21

"IS THIS supposed to be some kind of peace offering?" Jaime asked when Travis cooked enough dinner for both of them and then disappeared into his room with Alana without a word. It had only been a few days since he'd seen Jaime, but it felt longer. There was only so much he could figure out through texts and phone calls when Jaime insisted he was fine and Lupe was fine and everything in general was fine.

"Probably not."

"Is he worried you'll try to cook and burn down his kitchen? Because I wouldn't let you do that. Alana told me how many times you've burned popcorn." Jaime smirked at him and nudged Sean's calf with his foot before he went back to eating.

"He knows I'd just order food."

Jaime continued to eat for a few minutes in silence, but Sean had to hold back a smile as Jaime pushed his food around between bites and ran his hand over his head the same way he did when he couldn't decide what he wanted to do for one of his school projects. As impossible as it was to figure him out from a distance, it was getting easy to figure Jaime's thoughts out in person. Eventually, he sighed and kicked Sean in the shin.

"Fine. You're not going to volunteer it. Are you going to explain this to me if I just ask? Do you just want me to admit I care what he thinks? You already know that. He's your best friend. Of course I care what he thinks. I'm just pissed he thinks that extends to interfering with my life. So if it's not a peace offering, and it's not because he's just trying to keep you from cooking, what is it? Why did he make dinner for me? Is he trying to just fuck with my head?"

"For one thing, he's not an asshole. He wouldn't fuck with your head on purpose right now." Sean knew it came out harsher than it should have, but it wasn't the first time he'd had to point that out to someone, and he had kind of thought Jaime knew better.

"Sorry. I wasn't trying to insult him," Jaime said after a second. "I know he's a good friend to you. I just don't get him. He's pretty much shunned Lupe entirely. She's very upset about it. She texted him and offered to apologize for ever being rude to you, and he pretty much just told her not to talk to you. It's hard not to be pissed off at him for that. I know he wants to protect you, and it's not like I disagree with that. But then I get here and he just leaves without saying anything, but he makes me dinner. I don't get it. It feels like he's trying to make some kind of point, but I don't get it. So it feels like he's messing with me."

"Okay, but he's really not meaning to," Sean said as he pushed his own empty plate aside. He rested his hand on Jaime's left wrist and left it there after he felt some of the tension leave Jaime with his touch. "With Lupe, he's trying to protect me, and he also just doesn't like her opinion. He's doesn't want to give her the idea that her beliefs are excusable—which I know you disagree with, but you also know I agree with him, and I'm only putting up with her for you."

"So why the food?" Jaime said.

"You pretty much said he's not allowed to help, so I told him to back off. He's trying to respect that, but it bothers him. He likes to fix things or try to fix things or at least feel like he's doing something. So he made dinner. It's something he can do, so just let him do it, okay?"

Jaime was quiet for a few minutes before he nodded.

"Sure, okay."

"I should probably tell you that when I asked you to come here this weekend, it was because Alana wants to do something tomorrow morning, and while Travis doesn't have any other motives, she probably does."

"You didn't think you should tell me this before I was already here?" Jaime asked.

"I wanted you to come. I missed you."

"Stop with the pout." Jaime groaned, but his annoyed expression had melted.

"If you don't want to see her, I can get Travis to make her go away."

"I don't really want all your friends to hate me."

"None of my friends hate you. If they didn't like you, they wouldn't be so pushy."

"ALANA'S HERE!"

Sean groaned and rolled over in Jaime's arms so he could hide from the light in Jaime's chest.

"Alana says if you don't get up in ten minutes, she's coming in," Travis said through the door when he didn't answer.

"What time is it?" Sean mumbled.

Jaime pulled away enough to reach behind him to look at his phone.

"It's seven."

"Tell her to go away. She didn't say anything about waking me up when she said she wanted to hang out." Sean settled back in Jaime's arms and closed his eyes.

"Get up. I didn't tell you because you would have said no." Alana pounded on the door in between speaking. "Jaime, make him get up. I will come in there even if you're naked. You probably care. Sean doesn't. I've already seen him naked."

"Why has she seen you naked?" Jaime sat up even though Sean tried to pull him back down.

"Quick changes. She's just trying to get your attention."

"Jaime, I have coffee," Alana singsonged.

"Cheater!" Sean yelled, but he gave up pulling on Jaime's arm and let him get up to get dressed.

He'd just started to drift off again when Jaime came back in. His hand was still damp when he shook Sean's shoulder. When he leaned down to press his lips to Sean's cheek, Sean breathed in Jaime's scent mixed with his own body wash.

"Alana says she came over early because she knows how long it takes you to get ready. It would be nice if you started while I got dressed so I'm not trying to make small talk for half an hour. Also, I'm not new, and I know exactly what she's doing. I'm just pretending I don't because I want backup when I tell her I'm not going."

"If we're not going, why do I have to get ready?" Sean asked, but he sat up in bed after he opened his eyes and saw the tension on Jaime's face. "What does she want? I'll go out there and tell her we're not going. You can get back in bed. Why did you even get dressed for her?"

"I needed to think about it. The shower kind of cleared my head."

"Okay. So tell me what you think she wants, so I know what I'm up against. I promise I'll back you up, but it's Alana. She breaks down Travis on a regular basis. I need to at least know what I'm walking into."

"I think she wants us to go to church or mass with her." Jaime shrugged. "It's Sunday morning. She's dressed nice. It wasn't hard to figure out. Is she Catholic?"

"I don't know? I don't think so. I know her church is gay friendly."

"So probably not Catholic," Jaime said.

"Does that mean you're not allowed to go? Is that a rule? Am I allowed to go? I don't even really think I believe in God."

"You don't believe in God?" Jaime asked.

"Is that bad? It's not that I think you're wrong. I think it's possible. Maybe there's a God. Maybe there isn't." Sean shrugged. "Does it bother you that I don't care more? I mean, I care about your thoughts on it because it's important to you. I've just never really thought about it a lot."

"It's fine. I don't really want to think about it anyway—which is why I don't want to go. I know she's probably trying to help, but I don't want to go to a different church. I'm still Catholic—even if they don't want me."

"So we can tell her that." Sean slid out of the bed and picked up his T-shirt off the floor before finding pajama pants. There was no point in getting dressed when he was just going to drag Jaime back into bed.

"You already figured me out, didn't you?" Alana said when they stepped into the living room. Travis glanced at them from the other side of the kitchen counter, but he stayed quiet.

"Probably," Sean said. "We just came out to tell you we're going back to bed."

Alana turned all the way around on her stool to face them.

"I thought you might say that. You want coffee. I know you want coffee. Can you just hear me out over one cup of coffee?" She glanced at Sean, but she was clearly asking Jaime.

"Alana. If he doesn't want to go, you're not going to guilt him into it somehow."

"No guilt. Just listen, and then if you still don't want to go, I'll leave. I promise. I won't even use up all the time I planned to talk you into it and then factor in Sean taking an hour to get up and use every product in the bathroom. I won't even argue if you say no at the end of it."

"You always argue." Sean glanced at Jaime next to him. "It's up to you, but she's lying. She always argues."

"I won't. I promise," Alana said. "Besides, I explained this to Travis just now, and he also doesn't believe me. So I'm pretty sure he's going to jump in if I start arguing. So you'll have time to run. It'll be like the time I tried to talk you into getting a tattoo with me."

"You still ended up getting a tattoo," Sean pointed out.

"But you didn't."

Sean couldn't argue with that, so he just pulled Jaime aside into the hall by the bathroom.

"You don't have to listen. She's not even really going to be upset if you don't."

"I'll give her five minutes. She got up early and came all the way over here."

Jaime led them back to the kitchen, where Alana had already left a cup of coffee and a bagel in front of the seat next to her. Sean debated pushing it down the counter to the next place so he could put himself between them, but Jaime sat down before he could make a decision.

"Awesome." Alana smiled without the normal smirk he was used to, but Sean knew that was actually more dangerous. "So, I'm not trying to convert you or anything, I promise. I'm not trying to say my church is better, and you'll just decide you want to be Episcopalian. I know that's not how it is. I couldn't exactly go to a Catholic church and just decide that worked for me either. Maybe that's a bad example, but you get what I'm saying, right?"

Alana waited for Jaime to nod before she continued.

"I just think that it might be comforting for you to have a safe place to worship. I know you don't believe all the same things, but we're talking to the same God and reading the same Bible. We'll sit in the back, and you can only participate as much as you want. And I'm not going to pressure you to come back or come often, but you're always welcome. I know you haven't really been going to mass regularly anyway. I might not if my mom didn't guilt me every time I skip. But I know sometimes when things really suck, it helps me, so I wanted to offer." Alana paused to take a breath before she added, "Also, the plan was to make Sean come with you so if you ever want to talk to him, he'll have more of a clue what you're talking about. I think I lost him somewhere around saying I won't try to convert you. I don't think he's been inside a church when there wasn't a wedding."

"I've been inside churches," Sean said.

"Was it in Europe with a tour group?"

"Possibly."

"I just don't think I really want to answer questions from a lot of new people," Jaime said.

"You don't have to. I told my mom I was just going to sit with you guys and we'd probably skip the coffee hour. I can block anyone that tries to corner us. Plus, Sean's totally going to make us late anyway. We'll end up sneaking in right before the service."

"I don't really have nice clothes here."

"You can wear jeans. You won't even stick out. There's a lot of people who have jobs where they have to work Sundays, and they leave from mass."

Jaime turned away from her to look at him. Sean tried to figure out if this was his cue to refuse so Jaime didn't have to do it, but there was more of a question in Jaime's eyes than any plea to save him.

"Whatever you want to do," Sean said.

"Can we leave early if I want to?" Jaime asked Alana.

"Whenever you want."

SEAN STUDIED Jaime from his side of the bed as Jaime stared up at the ceiling. He was trying not to push, but other than the few words Jaime had exchanged with Alana after the service, he'd been quiet on the ride back to the apartment.

"Did you tell Alana you were glad you went just because you didn't want to make her feel bad?" Sean asked after a few minutes.

"No," Jaime said. "I'm not going to convert or go all the time, but she was right. It was nice."

"I don't really get it," Sean admitted when Jaime didn't explain. "Not that you have to explain it to me. You don't, but I might ask her about it. I'm going to avoid saying she was right about anything, because that's really going to make her gloat for months, but I do want to understand better."

"It's complicated."

"I got that. I didn't even get what was going on most of the time."

Jaime laughed and shook his head.

"I know you didn't just mean the service," Sean added. "But it might help me to start there. Don't worry, Alana won't care if I ask her all the dumb questions. She likes explaining things to me like I'm an idiot."

Jaime turned his head to smile at him, but he looked back to the ceiling before he spoke.

"It's kind of like she said this morning. It wasn't exactly the same as what I'm used to. But it was similar, and it was safe and just kind of going through the routine and listening to the same scriptures and the sermon. It's comforting."

"When you were gone and out of touch, Travis opened the studio for us. When I couldn't concentrate on anything new, he just made us run through a couple of my favorite older pieces that he still remembered because he remembers everything. It helped to just kind of go through something familiar and let everything out."

"Yeah. It's something like that. I can see that when you dance."

"Do you think Alana bribed them to do that poem thing?"

Jaime laughed before he said, "The Psalm? No. I actually asked her, but she said the scriptures are picked out far in advance for them, and they don't just skip around."

"So the whole part about how if your parents leave you, God will take you or something was just a really fitting coincidence? Because that's weird."

"I guess it depends on how you think about it," Jaime said.

$\mathcal{E}$PILOGUE

SEAN LEFT Alana and Travis outside with Aleksandra so he could enter the gallery alone. Aleksandra said she needed air before the opening reception officially started, but Jaime was already somewhere inside agonizing over his part of the exhibition. Sean knew he couldn't make any changes, but he was never going to believe it was perfect. Sean took his time moving past the pictures he'd already memorized from the nights he'd woken up alone in bed and watched Jaime sort through and edit each picture again and again until it told the right story.

Jaime was leaning against the wall by the final picture. Sean knew Jaime had taken it in the alley behind a motel. He'd gone to the motel planning to take pictures of Anastasia in the room, only to find her hiding outside after the guy she had met tried to insist on paying the second half of her fee with cocaine. There was a bruise visible on her wrist as she stomped out her cigarette with the toe of her red high heel. Jaime had wanted to just take her home, but Anastasia told him that if he was going to put all the work into changing his thesis exhibition in the last semester, he might as well tell the whole story.

"You're amazing," Sean said when Jaime turned to look at him. "This whole show is amazing."

"Thanks." Jaime pulled Sean against his side so they could look at the print together.

"So what's wrong?" Sean asked when Jaime kept staring at the same picture.

"I was hoping it would feel worth it."

"Worth it?"

"I got to do the show I wanted. My advisor said it beats all my other work. They're taking half of it to a gallery in the city for another exhibition, but Lupe isn't even coming."

"Do you regret everything?" Sean wasn't sure he wanted the answer, but he looked up to watch Jaime's face anyway.

"What?" Jaime's forehead crinkled with confusion for a second before his expression softened. "No, babe. That's not what I meant. It's just the exhibit. I wish they were here, and I was hoping seeing it all together would make it worth it that they weren't. That's all I meant."

"It's still amazing." Sean paused before adding, "You shouldn't give it up."

"I'm still taking the job I have," Jaime said, but the corner of his lip turned up as he pressed his lips to Sean's temple. "But I can work from home a lot already. I have time. I can see what happens."

Sean turned so they were face-to-face as the doors opened and people started flowing in from the other side of the gallery.

"For what it's worth, *I'm* proud of you. I'm so proud of you that I made Elizabeth and Eric plan their annual trip so they can catch your exhibit in the city. I also linked my parents to the gallery online. They're very impressed. They tried to talk me into letting them come. I just thought it would stress you out too much to deal with them right now," Sean said. "I know it's not the same, but I'm always going to be proud of you."

"Even if I end up taking passport photos for money?"

"You could probably make people look good in passport pictures. They'd probably pay a lot of money for that."

"You're ridiculous," Jaime said, but he laughed and pulled Sean into a hug.

"You love me."

"Yeah, yeah, I do," Jaime said, and then leaned down to brush his lips against Sean's neck as he whispered, "*Siempre te amaré.*"

"You've been saying that lately. Are you ever going to tell me what that means?"

"You could look it up. You looked up *te amo*," Jaime said as he pulled back. "Or you could ask Alana. It's one extra word. She probably knows it."

"I know, but I was hoping at some point you'd just want to tell me."

Jaime turned to look at the door, but almost everyone was still making their way through Aleksandra's exhibit at the front of the gallery. When he turned back, he gazed over Sean's shoulder at the picture behind them for a moment before meeting Sean's eyes.

"It means always. I love you always."

TESSA CÁRDENAS was born and raised in small town Texas, but she left on a greyhound the day she graduated high school. Tessa studied ballet for nine years before running away to join the circus where she took her skills into the air on the Spanish web and double trapeze. Since graduating from Florida State University, she has lived in San Francisco and Washington DC. She had an affair with New York City, but it would never commit, so she accepted a proposal from Chicago. At this point, it's possible she's not really from anywhere anymore.

In the free time she pretends to have between her day job and writing, Tessa volunteers for multiple LGBTQA organizations, studies pole dancing, and tries to get other lesbians to go out with her. Tessa can be found misbehaving on Twitter when she's supposed to be writing.

Also from TESSA CÁRDENAS

THE
STRONGEST
SHAPE

Tessa Cárdenas

http://www.dreamspinnerpress.com

Also from DREAMSPINNER PRESS

HOPE COVE
Brokenhearted

CATE ASHWOOD

http://www.dreamspinnerpress.com

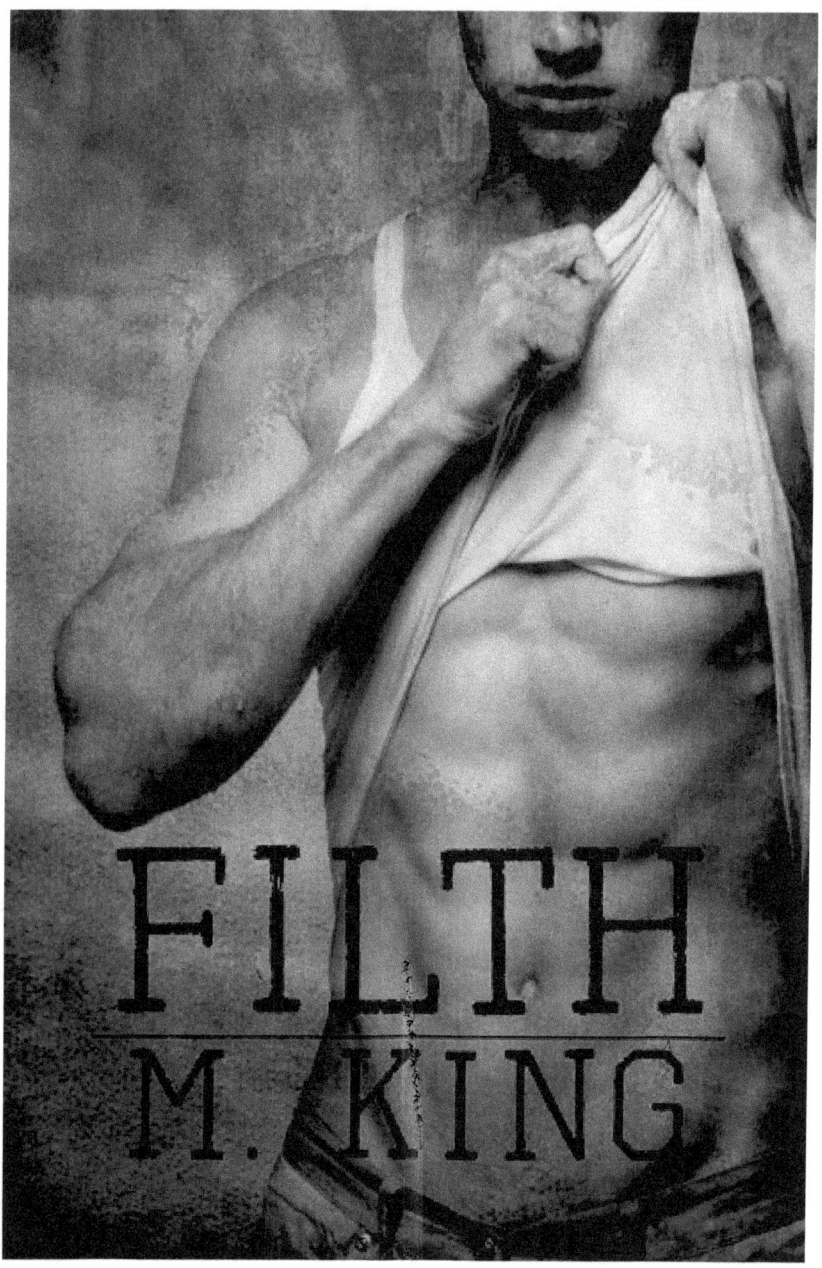

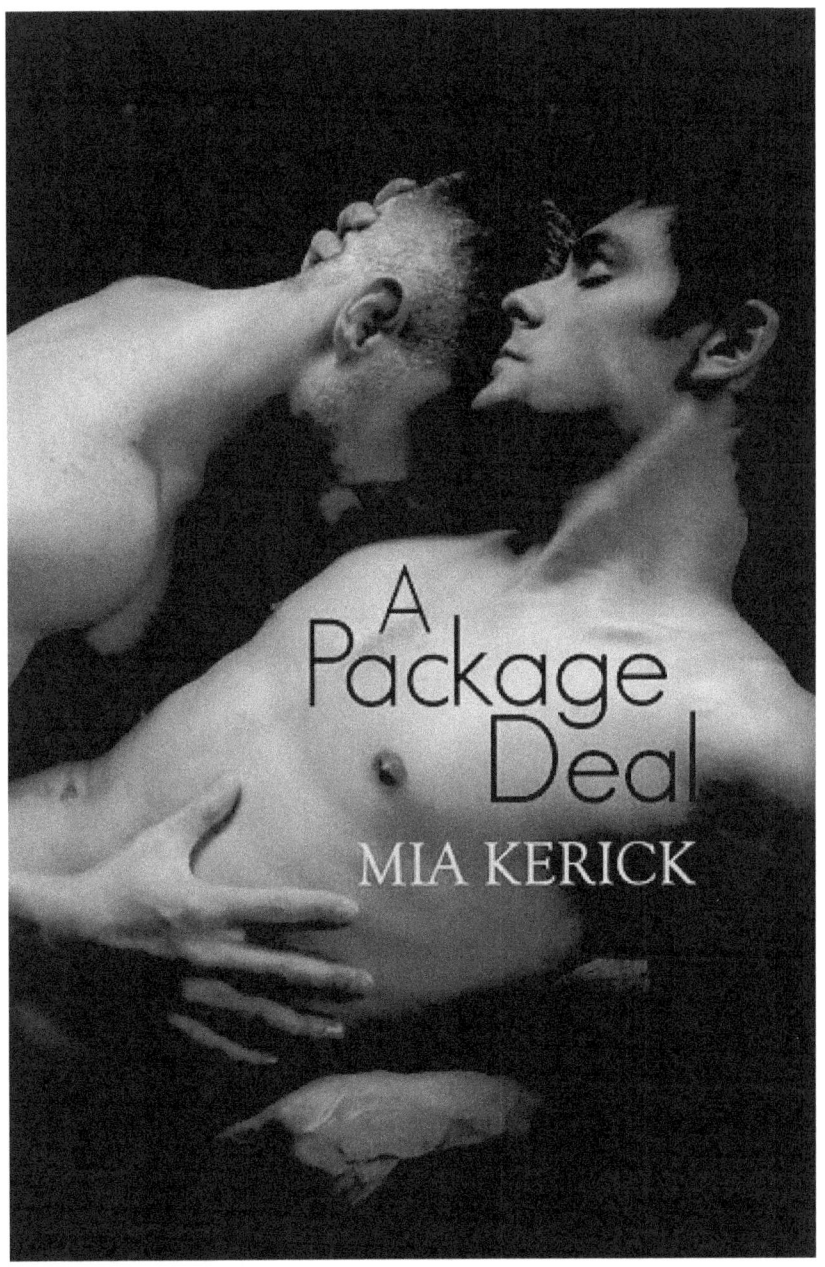

Irreversible eRROR

Wolf Phoenix

MORNING REPORT

SUE BROWN

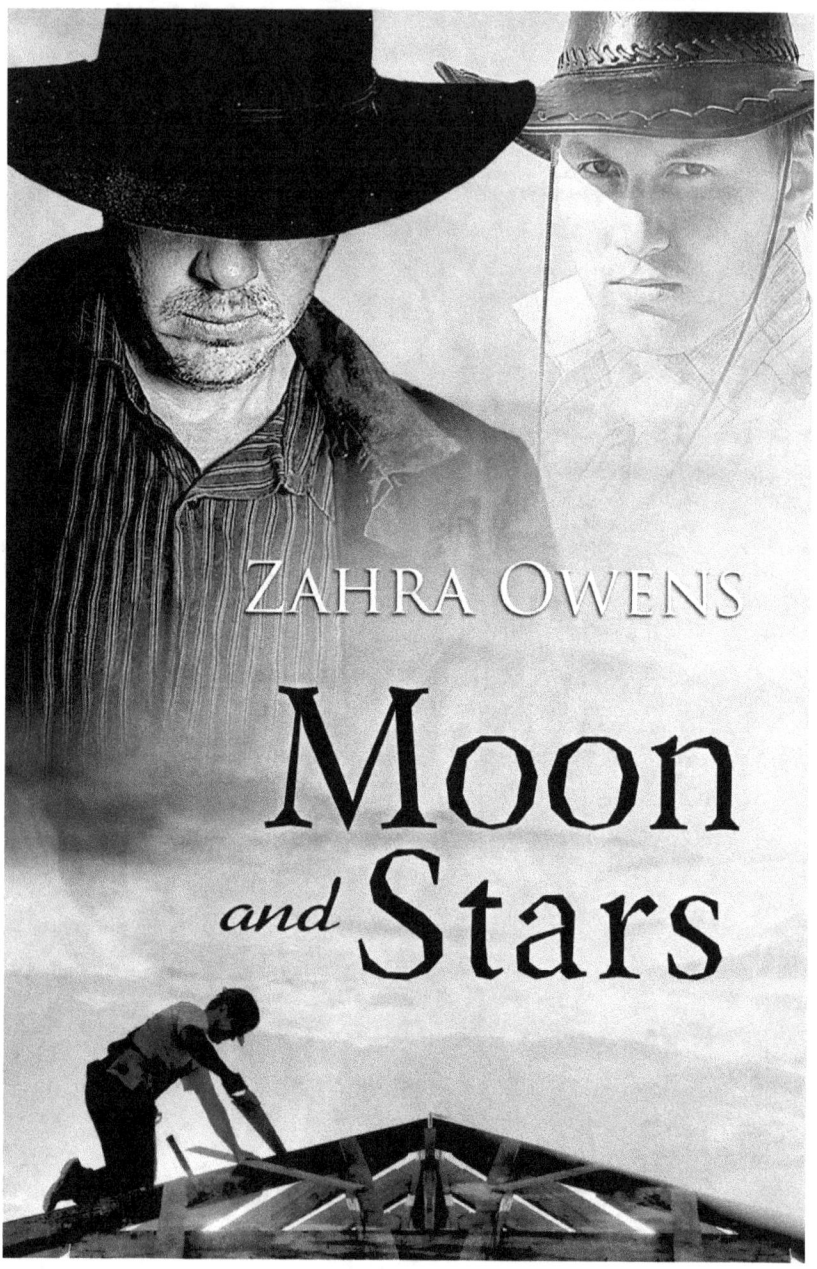